Three Versions of the Truth

Three Versions of the Truth

For Janice – A fellow
Nebraskan! What else
can I say, besides
"Go Big Red"? ☺

Amy Knox Brown

All best,
Amy Knox Brown

Press 53
Winston-Salem, North Carolina

Press 53

PO Box 30314

Winston-Salem, NC 27130

First Edition

Cover design by Kevin Watson

Cover photograph, "the last run [the day before]"
copyright © 2006 by Pivi Molinghen,
used by permission of the artist

"The Usual Punishment" appeared in *Punk Planet*

"The Slave Trade" appeared in *Shenandoah*

"Ray Sips a Low Quitter" appeared in *Missouri Review*, and in the
  anthology *High Infidelity: 24 Great Short Stories About
  Adultery* (William Morrow)

"Abandon" appeared in *Other Voices*

"Constellations" appeared in *Two Rivers Review*

"In the Field of Cement Animals" appeared in *Crab Orchard Review*

"Sitting Bull's Translator Remembers the Speech in Bismarck,
  N.D." appeared in the Raleigh (NC) *News and Observer*

"Why We Are the Way We Are" appeared in *Beloit Fiction Journal*

"Aeneas Leaves Kansas" appeared in *Narrative*

Printed on acid-free paper

ISBN 978-0-9793049-3-4

For my parents,
Larry and Carol Brown

History is the version of past events that people have decided to agree upon.

—Napoleon Bonaparte

Contents

Dr. Faustus in Lincoln

T he night before Halloween, on his way to a party, Dan
Morrow—wearing a suit that had belonged to his
grandfather and holding an old, leather-bound volume of
Christopher Marlowe's plays—paused on the sidewalk of Calumet
Court to take in the neighborhood's holiday decorations.
Scarecrows lounged like drunkards against the posts of yard lights.
Fat pumpkins sat on porches, carved with triangular eyes and
toothy grins, candles flickering inside their hollowed heads. Here
and there among the orange ones, a white pumpkin glowed. The
lack of color struck Dan as slightly ominous, unsettling. Albino
pumpkins, he thought. Where had the first one appeared? Had it
been a carefully cultivated mutation or a genetic freak?

Overhead, the branches of trees rustled and a yellow slice of
moon dangled in the sky.

Behind Dan, a car door slammed, and he heard his name:
"Danny! Danny-boy!" He turned to face Trent Mattson, an old
friend from high school who Dan hadn't seen in the fifteen years
since he left for college. "Trent," Dan said. "How're you doing?"

Trent was fine, his young features now padded over with a
layer of flesh, hairline beginning to recede. He wore a grizzly bear
suit with the bear head tucked under his arm; worn patches on the
chest gave him a mangy appearance.

"Who are you?" Trent lifted Dan's arm to read the spine of the
book. "Who's Christopher Marlowe?"

11

Dan explained that Marlowe was a Renaissance playwright, a contemporary of Shakespeare's, who was murdered under suspicious circumstances. He'd been stabbed in the eye.

Trent covered his own eye with a furry brown paw and said, "Ow."

Christopher Marlowe wrote a play called *Dr. Faustus*, about a professor at the University of Wittenberg who sold his soul to the Devil. And that was Dan's costume: he was Dr. Faustus.

Trent nodded. Dan could have elaborated about the character of Mephistopheles, that melancholy demon who functioned as Faustus' factotum, or about Faustus' pleasure at the trivial gifts he received for the sale of his soul. Dan wanted to quote from the scene at the end of the play, which he'd read just before leaving his apartment. When demons dragged Faustus down to hell, the doctor cried out, "Ugly hell, gape not, come not, Lucifer! I'll burn my books." Faustus must have been choking with fear, the demons' claws rending his skin, stench of sulfur on their breath. But Dan stopped talking before he lost his audience, a skill he used to good effect in his Introduction to Renaissance Literature classes. He stopped while Trent's expression remained affectionate and indulgent, as if he were thinking, *Danny, our very own intellectual. Our very own egghead.*

"Man, it's great you came home." Trent slapped Dan on the back. "I knew it was you the minute I saw you."

"Really?" Dan tried not to sound too pleased, but he found being remembered deeply comforting. He was recognized, even with his dark hair growing gray, and even after so much time had passed: after college and graduate school on the east coast, Dan had taken his first teaching job at the University of Virginia, and he'd been away from Nebraska for nearly half of his life. "Thanks, man."

Trent led the way to Gina Watson Shore's house. Inside, Gina hugged Dan. She wore a clown suit, a fright wig, and garish makeup. "I'm so glad you're here!" she said. "Everyone's so happy that you recovered your senses and came back to Lincoln—"

Well. Of course no one here saw Dan's situation—leaving the University of Virginia to take a job in the University of Nebraska's English department—as emblematic of failure. They didn't know that the potential of not getting tenure at UVA, combined with an unhappy romance with one of his better-published colleagues, was Dan's impetus for returning. They believed he came home from *desire*.

And they didn't know that Dan hadn't always been kind when he'd talked about his hometown and the people there. He'd used words like *provincial, predictable, set in their ways*. About Lincoln itself, he'd said *quiet, slow-paced, the opposite of cosmopolitan*. But the last part was *true*: sociologists had proven, after all, that trends took five years to travel from the coasts to the center of the country. Five years! So by the time men in Lincoln were wearing double-breasted suits, the same style filled Goodwill bins in New York City.

"Well," Dan said. "I'm glad to be back." Gina smelled of greasepaint and perfume. Her torso pressed heavy and solid against him, the way it had twenty years earlier when he'd hugged her after a Southeast Knights football game. "Gina," he said. "You haven't changed a bit."

The other guests crowded around him. Someone pushed a beer into his hand. There were questions about Dan's costume: Who was Dr. Faustus? Why did he sell his soul to the Devil?

"For knowledge," Dan said. "He wanted to know—everything."

The explanation received snorts of disdain, mutters of "bad deal." A pedestrian analysis, but correct, Dan had to admit. Faustus *had* made a bad deal when he sold his soul; he hadn't gotten the supreme knowledge he bargained for. Questions he asked remained unanswered. When he said to Mephistopheles, *Tell me, sweet devil, who made the world*, the demon had replied, *I will not*.

Gina tugged on Dan's sleeve and motioned for him to bend down so she could whisper in his ear. "Clare's here," she said. "She's back in town, too. Only for a little while, though."

Clare: his high school girlfriend. The first girl he'd had sex with, the first girl he'd said he'd loved. The girl he'd broken up with before he'd gone away to college.

"She lives in Iowa now," Gina continued, "but she and her husband are having some—problems, and she came home for a while to think things through."

And as if Gina's words had conjured her up, Clare walked toward him. She wore street clothes: a pair of faded jeans torn across the knees, a tight white sweater. Her hair was still long—past her shoulders—though a lighter color than he remembered. She held a beer. Up close, he saw fine lines tracing the corners of her eyes and slightly deeper lines on either side of her mouth. Looking at her face, still pretty but older, he felt a complicated mixture of attraction, nostalgia, and guilt.

"Danny." She raised the beer and tilted her head to one side, a distinct and familiar gesture. "The Prodigal Son returns." She gave him a hard, perfunctory hug and stepped back while his arms were still clasped around her.

He could have said, *I heard you're married;* or *I heard you're having problems;* or *I heard you live in Iowa.* Instead he asked, "Where's your costume?"

"This *is* a costume. I'm my old self. This was my favorite outfit in high school, don't you remember?"

"Your old self," he repeated. "That's a great idea."

"Who are you?"

"Dr. Faustus. He was a character in a play by Christopher Marlowe who—"

"I *know* who Dr. Faustus is," Clare said. "I was an English major."

Dan nodded. Of course Clare would have been an English major: she'd liked puns, crossword puzzles, stories. The connection with language was what had drawn them together in high school. How many afternoons had he sat across from her in the library, watching her bite gently on the top of her pen as her eyes scanned the pages of books?

How odd to see her in the same old clothes, as if nothing had changed.

Clare said, "'Think on hell, Faustus, for thou art damned!'"

"Am I?" Dan asked. He found himself gazing into her eyes. Contact lenses rested on her brown irises.

"I don't know," she said. She took the book from him and flipped through the fragile pages. "My favorite part was the scene with the Seven Deadly Sins. You know the one I mean?"

"Of course," Dan said. For Faustus' entertainment—and to distract him from thinking about God and reconsidering his decision to sell his soul—Lucifer and Beelzebub had presented him with a pageant of the Seven Deadly Sins, each of whom spoke to Faustus and described their dispositions: *I am Envy... I cannot read and therefore wish all books were burnt. I am lean with seeing others eat.*

Hey ho, I am Sloth. I was begotten on a sunny bank where I have lain ever since, and you have done me great injury to bring me from thence. Let me be carried thither again...

"I *love* the Seven Deadly Sins."

"All of them?" He thought of the Deadly Sin of lust; he remembered pressing his lips against the back of Clare's neck, how she would moan and go limp against him.

"Well, some more than others." She smiled. Dan smiled back. Their breakup was apparently of no consequence tonight. Clare began ticking the Deadly Sins off on her fingers: Lust, envy, sloth, wrath, greed, covetousness—

"Greed and covetousness are the same," Dan said.

She narrowed her eyes at him, then continued, "So after greed, we have gluttony, and then the deadliest of the Deadly Sins, pride."

Pride was the deadliest sin because a prideful person believed himself to be the center of the universe. A prideful person thought he was more important than God, the worst possible notion someone could entertain, according to Renaissance doctrine.

From the stereo, the Cars sang: *I don't mind you coming here and wasting all my time time,* a song Dan first heard on New Year's Eve of 1979. Cigarette smoke rose in the air; Gina moved among the guests, freshening drinks, nudging conversations along. Clare went to the kitchen for two more beers, and when she returned, Dan said, "So tell me about your husband."

The crowd swirled around them. Somebody said, "Those white pumpkins give me the creeps—they seem like, I don't know, *possums.*"

"He's in Iowa," Clare said. "I have a theory. About the Seven Deadly Sins. I think everyone has a personal Deadly Sin, psychologically speaking. Sort of like the way people are introverted or extroverted?"

Dan drank from his fresh beer. "Go on."

"Me, for example; I'd have to say my personal Deadly Sin is wrath. I get too pissed off about things."

"What about Trent's?"

"Sloth," Clare said, without hesitation. "He's not very motivated."

Dan nodded. "What about Gina?"

Clare made a face, the expression of someone forced by honesty to say something meaner than she wanted. "Probably gluttony. But Gina's a wonderful person—"

"I know."

"What about you? What's your sin?"

It could be any number of things, Dan thought: sloth, for his failure to publish a book; envy, for the jealousy he felt toward people who *did* publish books; and there was always despair, considered to be the eighth Deadly Sin, the sin that plagued Hamlet.

"Faustus' sin was pride," Clare said. "Is that yours, too?"

"God, I hope not," Dan said, though a visceral twinge, the sensation of unconscious knowledge brought to the surface, reverberated behind his ribs. "I'll take envy."

Clare shrugged. "Suit yourself."

❧

Hours passed. Dan drank a third beer, a fourth. Trent handed him a shot of tequila and he threw it back, grimacing. He examined pictures of his classmates' children; he nodded sympathetically at the story of Trent's divorce. "She said I didn't do enough to keep the relationship *alive*," Trent said. In one hand, he held the bear head by the ear; he'd never put it on.

Dan thought: Clare was right. Trent was sloth.

In high school, parties had lasted until two or three in the morning, but now people needed to get home to relieve babysitters, to rest up for mornings full of yard work, shopping, family obligations. A little past midnight, the rooms began to clear. Gina approached Dan. Her fright wig hung slightly askew, so her head appeared tilted. "Can you give Clare a ride home?" she asked. "She's pretty drunk—I don't think she should drive."

"Sure," Dan said. "No problem."

In the months and years after this particular Halloween, Dan tried to reconstruct precisely what had happened after he walked outside with Clare. She leaned against him as they moved down the front steps. The balmy air held an undercurrent of chill. From porches, the flickering eyes of jack-o'-lanterns watched them. The albino pumpkins glowed white as skulls.

After they got into Dan's car, there's a blank space of time. He was driving. Who suggested taking a memory-soaked tour down Twenty-Seventh Street to Saltillo Road? Who wanted to turn into the lot behind Wilderness Park, where, in high school, they'd left weeds around the lot's perimeter marked with condoms?

Does it matter who made the suggestion? If Dan made the suggestion, is he more complicit in what he now knows had happened?

Dan parked in the northwest corner, the same spot they'd been when he broke up with Clare. That night, while they were having sex, he thought nostalgically *last time, last time* and almost reconsidered his decision. But no, he'd told himself; he had to be resolute. Afterwards, while they shared a cigarette, he said, "You know, I think we should see other people." Her face had turned toward his, her features frozen with shock.

It had been spring then, a few weeks before high school graduation, new leaves sprouting on the branches of trees that now, two seasons removed and fifteen years later, hung bare in the illumination of headlights. A gust of wind buffeted the car. Clare slid closer to Dan and shut off the ignition. She used to do that: reach over while he was driving and turn on the windshield wipers if rain started, or honk the horn when someone ahead of them at a stoplight didn't accelerate quickly enough. It drove him crazy, the sudden movements of her hands in his personal space.

She put her hand on his leg.

"Are you mad at me, that we broke up?" Dan asked.

"We haven't broken up," she said.

"What?"

"We haven't broken up," she repeated. "I'm my old self, I don't even know it's going to happen."

"What about your husband?"

"What husband?" She tilted her head. "I'm only seventeen, I don't have a husband."

She was drunk; Dan knew that. Still, he turned his face to hers. The perfectly familiar way her mouth moved against his made the years between then and now recede, then vanish. The soft sweater he'd touched in high school, her ribs, still sharp, her hair sliding against his face. Their knees creaked like old people's knees as they shifted and squirmed out of their clothes.

He slid into the passenger seat. Clare straddled his legs, holding herself slightly above him, looking at his face and smoothing the skin under his eyes with her thumbs. "Old Danny," she said. "Still as handsome as ever." She lowered her hips. Dan slid inside her. He closed his eyes. "Oh," she whispered. "It's just the same, isn't it?"

"The same," he said. He braced his feet against the car's floor. Her hips dipped and rose. His fingers pressed into the flesh of her thighs. She whispered in his ear, *Slow down. I'm close.*

Opening his eyes momentarily, Dan saw the same trees he'd looked at years ago, the sky beyond the windshield blank as a chalkboard, untouched with stars. She was her old self, and who was he? A boy, unknowing? The Prodigal Son, returned? Or Dr. Faustus, safe and ignorant in the days before the Devil came to claim his due?

Now, Clare whispered. She ground her hips against him. *Now.*

On Monday, Dan met Clare for lunch at Barrymore's, a dark bar at the back of the Stuart Theatre. They ordered cheeseburgers and beer.

The waitresses in Barrymore's wore black and white clothes; the bar itself was located in the backstage area of the theater, where the ceiling soared forty feet above their heads. The bathrooms, upstairs, were built into old dressing rooms. The bathroom floors consisted of black and white hexagonal tiles fitted together precisely as teeth. Barrymore's was a nice bar, a cosmopolitan sort of place. You could bring a visitor from New York here and not be embarrassed.

Dan mentioned this to Clare when he came back downstairs. She'd ordered more beer; it glowed amber in the tall glasses. "You did bring a guy from New York here," she said. "Over Christmas break, first year of college. Don't you remember?"

Dan sipped his beer. His first semester at BU had turned out to be more difficult than he'd expected, and so he avoided thinking about his freshman year. By now it seemed that all the neglected, unthought-of, pushed-aside remembrances had dissolved. Who would he have invited home to Lincoln, anyway? Who from out east would have wanted to spend their holiday here in the snowy Midwest?

He shook his head. "I don't remember."

She sighed, exasperated. "It was a guy who lived in your dorm. Not your roommate, I don't think. His name was—" She paused and tapped her index finger against her lip. "*William*. And he called you *Daniel*. He was from New York City, and you were so impressed by that, you kept mentioning it every five minutes—" She breathed deeply, as if to calm herself. The way she'd said the names, in a ringing, pretentious tone, though, reminded Dan. He'd been friends with William only during the first semester of freshman year. William had flown to Iowa to visit his grandparents for Christmas. Since Lincoln was only three hours from Des Moines, William rented a car and drove to Lincoln to spend the weekend with Dan, and when Dan brought William to Barrymore's—he'd heard they didn't card—they'd run into Clare and some other people from high school.

Dan said, "Who all was here?"

"Me. Gina and Trent and Brian. Trent had just broken up with Kelly, and so he was kind of mopey and drinking a lot."

"Right," Dan said. "He wanted to get married, and then he found out she was dating someone else."

Clare nodded. "Who in their right mind wants to get married in college—but that's Trent. Anyway, your friend, this William, kept buying him shots, and at first I thought it was a nice gesture, but then I figured William was just trying to get Trent drunk out of his mind. As a kind of experiment or something." She narrowed her eyes at Dan. "People die from drinking too much, you know."

What exactly was she getting at? Dan wished he remembered the night more clearly so he could adopt the right tone. He felt defensive, but maybe he was taking things too personally.

"William kept going on and on about how much there is to do in New York. You can go to the theater, you can go to restaurants, and beautiful women everywhere you look—" Clare tilted her head side to side, theatrically, as she talked.

That almost-forgotten night hadn't turned out well, Dan thought. He motioned for the waitress to bring them another round.

"And then he said, 'You know, Daniel, the girls in Lincoln are pretty enough, but they have a certain corn-fed look. They're all about twenty pounds too heavy to be attractive by New York standards.'"

Dan looked down at the table.

"You knew Gina was sensitive about her weight, and she was crushed, just crushed, and when Trent tried to defend us—us girls, I mean—he was so drunk he couldn't talk, and William started making fun of him. Making fun of him being drunk, and saying he should be glad that his ex-corn-fed fatty was off boning somebody else." Clare cleared her throat. "Boning somebody else, that's exactly what he said."

Surely, Dan told himself, he'd risen to the occasion, he'd stood up to William and told him to watch his mouth. Surely he'd done that.

"And *you,*" Clare continued. The waitress set down fresh beers, picked up the empty glasses, and retreated.

Dan had forgotten what happened that night almost fifteen years earlier, and he'd forgotten some things about Clare that this conversation brought back. She'd always been a little high-strung, prone to inexplicable fits of anger. Her personal Deadly Sin *was* wrath, he thought. Also, she tended to drink too much. He remembered now.

"And you just sat there, with this simpering grin on your face—"

"Simpering?" Dan said, stung.

She took a long drink of beer. "Anyway, I don't know why I let myself get so mad about something that happened so long ago."

"Hey," Dan said. He kept his tone light. "You can't help it— it's just wrath, your personal Deadly Sin."

For a second, he thought he'd made things worse, but then she laughed. "And how! Just my personal Deadly Sin—it's the perfect excuse."

"Well, if it's any comfort," Dan continued, "William flunked out of school at the end of the year." He was lying; he had no idea what happened to William.

"Good," Clare said. "Serves him right, the pretentious *jerk*."

Dan thought he'd repaired the rift—if there had been a rift—though he wasn't sure if he wanted to see her again; rekindling a romance with a married high school girlfriend was foolhardy, especially now that he remembered how volatile Clare could be. They finished their beers peacefully, then Dan paid the bill and they left the bar. On the walk to Clare's car, the sky hung overhead, heavy with clouds, and a breeze—oddly warm, for the beginning of November—pressed against their faces. The low sky and warm wind made the afternoon feel incongruous and unsettling, like white pumpkins among the orange ones.

"Who invented white pumpkins?" Dan asked.

Clare shook her head. "I don't know." She reached in her coat pocket and pulled out her car keys. Dan leaned forward to kiss her goodbye and she turned her head so that his lips touched her cheek. Of course: she was married; she couldn't stand on a busy street kissing a man who wasn't her husband.

Or else she was still angry with him. Dan suppressed a sigh.

"Bye, Danny," Clare said. She had on sunglasses, so he couldn't see her eyes. "Thanks for lunch."

On Friday, Dan and Trent lurked through the aisles at Barnes and Noble. Trent had heard that bookstores were the new singles bars; he'd convinced Dan to assist him—to play Mephistopheles to Trent's Faustus, Dan thought wryly—because Trent needed advice on exactly where he should browse to find the right sort of woman. Besides, bookstores made Trent nervous, he admitted. He didn't want to go in one by himself.

Against the back wall of the store stood a shelf of poetry books. "Poets can be—free-spirited," Dan said. "But kind of crazy." Trent shook his head. "No crazy."

They paused by a table of new releases. A tall, dark-haired woman studied the titles. She glanced at them and smiled. Trent opened his mouth as if to speak, then noticed the diamond ring winking on her left hand. His shoulders slumped.

"Come on, buddy," Dan said. He steered Trent toward the classical fiction section. "Don't give up so easily."

Trent stopped in the self-help aisle. The books' titles were alternately accusatory and encouraging: *Take Control of Control Freaks!—Whose Fault is it?: How Birth Order Dooms and Frees You—Daily Meditations for your Positive Journey through Life.*

"Jenna loved these things." Trent pulled *Daily Meditations* off the shelf. "She thought they really could help solve your problems."

Dan was on the verge of delivering a lecture: if Trent was standing around in the self-help section, the only sort of woman he was likely to meet was a woman with *problems*. Furthermore, these books contained nothing but claptrap. The authors took some sort of gimmick and dressed it up in psychology. Something ridiculous, like "how theories of horse training can help you understand your marriage." He'd said, "Trent," when it occurred to him that maybe Trent *liked* the sort of woman who read self-help books. Dan ought to consider Trent's needs, instead of assuming that Trent's taste was identical to Dan's, that Trent wanted a woman with intellectual glasses and an appreciation for Marlowe.

Trent looked up from the book. His expression was mild and puzzled; he must have been thinking about his ex-wife. "Yeah?"

"Can you hand me that one on control freaks?" Dan asked.

"Sure."

The cover of *Take Control of Control Freaks* boasted *Tens of thousands of copies in print! Four weeks on the* New York Times *extended bestseller list!* Dan opened the book and began reading. *Ellen's boss Jean was a particularly toxic sort of control freak. Jean continually undermined Ellen's self-esteem by—*

"Hey," Trent said. "Thanks for coming with me tonight."

"No problem, buddy," Dan said, relieved that he'd bitten his tongue. How judgmental he would have sounded if he'd gone on about the self-help books, how pompous and prideful.

Pride. That was his personal Deadly Sin, wasn't it? A shortcoming Dan struggled to overcome, the very reason people bought these ridiculous books in an effort to contend with their own foibles, like overeating (gluttony) or sexual addiction (lust).

And as the lights buzzed overhead and sounds of espresso-making hissed from the café, an idea descended into Dan's brain, with a jolt as physical as if someone had pinched him. *He* could write one of these books based on the personal Deadly Sins! He could tie together Marlowe's play with contemporary aspects of psychology, so the readers of *his* book would receive a little dose of Renaissance literature along with their self-help.

"I need a couple of these," Dan said. "What are some good ones?"

Trent selected titles he recognized from the stack on Jenna's bedside table.

"Thanks," Dan said, and carried the slippery pile toward the cash register.

Dan stayed up until three that morning reading about control freaks. Abominable prose, he thought, though he had to admit that he found useful suggestions for dealing with difficult people. *Detach yourself. Breath deeply and let your mind go blank.*

He must have dreamed about his own book, because when he woke after four hours of sleep, he knew the book's structure. Eight chapters—the Seven Deadly Sins plus the eighth Deadly Sin of despair. Each chapter opening with Marlowe's description from the parade of Deadly Sins in *Dr. Faustus*. For the Deadly Sin of despair, he'd use something from *Hamlet*. Then anecdotal examples, followed by psychological analysis—he'd need to check out some psych books from Love Library—and, finally, advice for taming the sin. *If you're feeling depressed, consult with a therapist to discuss your options for treatment.* Easy stuff, Dan thought. His mind brimmed with complete sentences, complete paragraphs, entire pages that he was compelled to type out on his computer. He felt, in fact, possessed.

Do you often sense that something is holding you back from achieving total satisfaction in your life? Some small, gnawing problem that keeps you awake at night, trying to determine exactly what it is? Perhaps the key to your difficulties lies in a theory that's based on notions we've studied for hundreds and hundreds of years, the idea of the seven Deadly Sins. Sloth, envy, wrath, pride, greed, gluttony, lust—each of us suffers from a personal Deadly Sin, the one thing that prevents us from becoming a fully actualized person. Join Christopher Marlowe and Dr. Faustus as they lead you on a journey to help you identify your personal Deadly Sin and offer suggestions on how to conquer it!

Dan spent two weeks in a state of feverish inspiration. While teaching, he thought constantly about his book, how he'd incorporate the quote he was discussing at that moment—for instance, Hamlet's "Oh, that this too too sullied flesh would melt,/ Thaw, and resolve itself into a dew!"—into the text. He titled his book *Who's Your Demon?* He sent query letters to agents when he finished the first hundred pages. He wondered—his energy surging as he sat typing into the early morning hours—if he suffered from manic depression.

Dan had finished a draft of *Who's Your Demon?* when he ran into Gina in Ideal Grocery two days before Thanksgiving. Shoppers crowded the store, stocking up for the approaching holiday; Gina's own cart brimmed with bags of potatoes, rolls, and breadcrumbs, cans of cranberry sauce and pumpkin, a huge turkey. They paused to talk for a minute in the produce aisle so Gina could fill Dan in on the latest news. Trent was dating someone, a woman who worked at Lee Bookseller. He'd met her when he went there to pick up a book his mother had ordered.

"She was two years behind us in high school," Gina said. "Betsy Wetlaufer?"

Dan shook his head; he didn't know her. "Good for Trent."

Gina agreed. The other news she had was that Clare had gone back to Iowa.

"Oh," Dan said. He swung his cart to one side to allow an elderly woman to pass. "Well, good, I'm glad that things worked out for her."

How much did Gina know? Dan wondered. She knew they left the party together. But did Clare tell her about the episode in Wilderness Park? He gazed at Gina over the mound of food. She met his eyes, then Dan looked away. He picked up a cantaloupe and held it toward her. "I've never been able to figure this out. How can you tell when these things are ripe?"

At the English department's holiday party, Dan met a graduate student, Jane Kreji. She was in the Ph.D. program, specializing in Plains Literature; she had long, curly red hair, pale freckled skin, eyes the color of pennies.

"I heard you finished a book," she said.

Dan shrugged, modestly. It was easy to be modest when four agents were presently looking at his manuscript to decide if they wanted to offer representation. "It's kind of silly, really, a combination of *Dr. Faustus* and pop psychology."

"It sounds fascinating," Jane said. "Tell me about it." She talked with her hands, and Dan noticed the skin across her knuckles was weathered, the sort of skin you'd expect to see on an older woman.

Later that night, he and Jane lay on his mattress in a dim pool of light from the bedside lamp. Against the pale flesh of her torso, Jane's hands appeared even more aged. She noticed Dan looking at them, and explained: she grew up in western Nebraska helping her father on his ranch, long summer days spent tending the cattle in the endless fields, pitchforking heavy bales of hay off the back of the pickup truck, hot hours of weeding the big garden behind the house. She'd always worn a hat to protect her face; but now she knew she should have worn gloves, too.

"Hindsight's always twenty-twenty, right?" Dan said. Months later, he would remember saying this, how ridiculous the cliché turned out to be, as if you really could see back into the past and understand fully what had happened.

In the cold days of January, Dan and Jane took walks in the afternoon. Packed snow squeaked under their feet. Sometimes Jane made dinner, steaming pots of stew or chili. Dan studied her while she stood in front of the stove. In profile, she reminded him of a mural he'd seen in the state capitol law library. The mural portrayed a pioneer woman staring pensively into the flat distance of Nebraska, an invisible breeze teasing her hair. Jane wore that same expression while she cooked, and Dan decided her personal Deadly Sin was probably despair.

He wrapped his arms around her and she turned toward him. He whispered her name. She smiled, her serious look dissolving: Dan held the power to make her happy.

An agent named Mary Phillmore called Dan. She worked with one of the big agencies in New York; she loved his book and was certain she could sell it quickly for a decent amount of money. Could she sign him on?

"Sure," Dan said. He sat in his office in the English department, pressing the phone cord into the desk. Hard pellets of snow smacked against the windows.

"I'll fax you a contract this afternoon, and then get together a list of publishers. I'm going to pitch the book as 'a masterful combination of Cliffs Notes and *Who Moved My Cheese?*' What do you think of that?"

In Virginia, Dan would have been humiliated by the mention of Cliffs Notes, and his colleagues would have laughed him out of the state. Here, however, things were different. In fact, Cliffs Notes originated in Lincoln, Nebraska; the Cliffs Notes office was a few blocks from campus; and a picture of Cliff Hillegass—entrepreneurial alumni who donated generous sums of money to the university—hung in Love Library. "I'm not sure it's a *Who Moved My Cheese?* kind of book," Dan said.

There was a pause.

"Doesn't matter," Mary Phillmore finally said. "*Who Moved My Cheese?* sold millions and millions of copies. You want the editors to sit up and take notice."

Dan cleared his throat. "Oh."

Academic publishing moved slowly, what with the peer reviews and lengthy requirements for readers' reports, so Dan was startled when Mary Phillmore called him two weeks after their first conversation and said, "I got you an offer from Cyclops Press." Cyclops: it was a respectable enough house that focused on self-help and commercial fiction. The colophon was a round face containing a single eye and slightly leering mouth.

"Cyclops," Dan said. "That's great!"

"The offer's not as high as I hoped, but not unreasonable, either. Low six figures." She mentioned the exact sum, and Dan's legs jerked involuntarily, sending his chair rolling back from his desk.

"That's—that's fine," Dan said. "Really, thanks a lot for all your work—"

"I'll mail you the contract as soon as I get it, which you'll need to sign and return immediately," Mary Phillmore said. "Cyclops wants the book out in time for Christmas, so things need to move pretty quickly from here on out. I'll be in touch."

Dan sat staring out the window for a long time after he hung up the phone, at the gray sky and piles of old snow. Students bundled in coats and scarves trudged along the walkways, their shoulders slumped under the doomed sense that winter would never end.

Six figures, Dan thought. Six figures!

But the snow melted, as it always did. The days grew longer. In the warming afternoons of spring, Dan addressed the queries of copy editors. He began writing a paper entitled "Hamlet and Faustus Pursue a Liberal Education: Was Wittenberg the first Berkeley?" Leaves unfurled on the branches of trees. Sometimes when Dan stood in a spot he'd been years ago—the sidewalk in front of Southeast High, for instance—he felt the presence of his younger self, as if the boy he'd been had walked up and was standing, silent, next to him. When his advance arrived, Dan bought a house a few blocks from Gina's, in the same neighborhood where he and his friends had grown up. Summer evenings, he and Jane strolled along the brick paths of the Sunken Gardens, holding hands. They peered into the pools where giant goldfish broke the water's surface and moved their mouths, as if whispering secrets.

And then Halloween arrived again, Dan's second Halloween back
in Lincoln. How had time passed so quickly? he wondered. He
stared in the mirror above his dresser, adjusting his tie. From the
bathroom, Jane called, "What time are we supposed to be there?"

"Oh, nine or so," Dan said. "Whenever."

She came out, dressed in a floaty pink dress she found at the
Junior League Thrift store. The style was clearly from the 1920's;
she'd done something so her hair looked bobbed, and she held a
long cigarette holder in one hand. "I need to get a cigarette to put
in this thing," she said. "So it looks authentic."

She pressed herself next to Dan and they regarded themselves
in the mirror: Scott and Zelda Fitzgerald, a commonplace disguise
in English departments, Dan supposed, but he suspected they'd
be the only pair of Fitzgeralds at Gina's party. He'd greased his
hair back to resemble Fitzgerald's in the author photos on Scribner
paperbacks. The suit he wore, an old one of his father's, smelled
faintly of mothballs and Old Spice.

This year, Gina was dressed as Barbara Bush, with a white wig
and a double strand of pearls around her neck. Was the costume
ironic or in homage? Dan wondered. He didn't ask. He moved
through the crowded rooms, his hand on Jane's—Zelda's—back,
introducing her. "Good to meet you," his old classmates said to
Jane. "Glad Danny's finally settling down." It turned out Jane
knew Betsy, Trent's girlfriend from the bookstore. "Small world!"
Trent said and slapped Dan on the back.

Dan had been there a while when he realized he hadn't seen
Clare. Of course, who would drive all the way from Iowa for a
Halloween party? The only reason she'd been here last year was
that fight with her husband, he thought. Still, once she crossed his
mind, he found himself thinking that it would be good to catch up,
to make sure she harbored no regrets about the clumsy encounter
in the car, no hard feelings about the disagreement in Barrymore's.
He stopped Gina on her way to the kitchen. "Mrs. Bush," he said.
"Might I ask you a question?"

She smiled at him; Gina loved people who got into the spirit of things. "Certainly, young man."

He dropped the phony, booming voice he'd adopted. "I was just thinking about Clare—I haven't seen her since last year, and I wondered how she was doing—"

Gina's face went blank, and then she looked him right in the eye. "Well, you know," she said, "she's pretty busy, with the new baby and everything."

"Baby?" Dan said. He felt himself blinking in surprise.

"A little girl, Emma," Gina continued.

"A baby," Dan repeated. "I didn't know—" He swallowed. "When?"

"Three months ago."

"Three months," Dan said. The way Gina was looking at him—did that mean something? If the baby was three months old, then she was born in August. And if she was born in August, then Clare must have gotten pregnant about a year ago.

A year ago. The last time he'd seen her.

Did that mean—?

Gina began speaking, in a rush. "She's darling, the baby, I mean. They were worried about her at first, because she was so small when she was born, not even five pounds, but she's gained a lot of weight and the doctors say she's perfectly healthy. Clare and Desmond couldn't be happier—"

"Desmond," Dan said. Clare had never mentioned her husband's name.

"That's his last name. Their last name. Clare and Steve Desmond."

"I didn't know," Dan said. His thoughts roiled around inside his head, like potatoes in a pan of boiling water. *Was* Gina acting strangely about the baby, or was Dan imagining things? Surely the baby—Emma—wasn't *his* baby. Clare would have told him. Wouldn't she?

Or would she? Later that night, Dan lay in bed next to Jane, who was asleep. His heart pounded; his feet were cold and sweaty. Last Halloween, Dan had been Dr. Faustus and Clare was her old self. He thought of Faustus and his devil Mephistopheles. *Tell me*, Faustus had begged. *Sweet Devil, tell me.*

The most palatable option, the easiest one to accept, was that the baby was not his baby. He constructed a story to support this thesis: Last year, Clare went home to her husband, and they decided to patch up their marriage and have a child. Dan knew people did things like that, expecting a life-altering event like pregnancy to overshadow all the ill-will and missed connects preceding it. The baby would show everyone that they were *starting fresh.*

That was the kind of easy, closed, sentimental narrative people liked. Dan himself liked this narrative; it absolved him of all responsibility, and it gave Clare a happy ending.

He rolled over. He closed his eyes. His lids, like tugged window shades, snapped open.

Of course, he'd find the happy-ending hypothesis easier to accept if Gina hadn't been acting so suspiciously, if the timing didn't make Dan slightly uneasy.

Dan forced himself to consider the alternate story: Dan and Clare have sex. No talk of birth control. Even as they argue in Barrymore's, Clare is pregnant. She stays in Lincoln until she discovers this fact, and then she returns to Iowa to resume her married life where she'll pass the baby off as her husband's.

It sounded Machiavellian. Machiavellian, but possible.

And speaking of possibilities—Dan acknowledged that a third option existed. Next to him, Jane sighed in her sleep. It was possible that Clare left Lincoln shortly after their lunch, returned to Iowa, slept with her husband, and so even Clare herself might not have been able to say with certainty who the father was.

Staring off into space, thinking, Dan heard Jane, as if from a distance, saying, "Dan? Is everything okay?"

"I'm fine," he replied. His voice held a false, jovial note, the same note that he'd struck for months in Virginia before he left.

But then the galleys of *Who's Your Demon?* arrived. The cover was white with the title written in a heavy black print, and the letter *n* at the end of the word *Demon* curved off into a pointy devil's tail. Below the title, *Dan Morrow, Ph.D.* in the same heavy print. The Cyclop's publicist called Dan almost daily to report on the book signings and radio interviews she'd scheduled. "I'm talking to Oprah's people, too," the publicist said. "Keep your fingers crossed."

Dan kept his fingers crossed. He dutifully recorded the upcoming events in his day planner. He handed out galleys to his colleagues in the English department. Would the other professors be interested? Dan wondered. Or would they think he'd embarked on a ridiculous project?

His musings were answered a few days later when Dan sat in his office, grading a stack of essays. *Marlowe was the greatest writer who ever lived, bar none, no argrument here.* Dan circled the misspelled word. He wrote, "This might be a difficult thesis to prove" in the margin. And then he was gratified to overhear his colleagues bantering with each other in the hall: *I'm feeling a little slothful about grading those composition essays.*

I indulged the sin of gluttony at lunch.

Someone's been a little greedy in the community cookie jar.

The week before Thanksgiving, exactly one year after he'd finished *Who's Your Demon?*, Cyclops Press sent Dan fifty copies of his book. A UPS guy wheeled the heavy box up to his office. "Thanks," Dan said. He carefully cut the tape that held the package shut. His hands, he noticed, trembled slightly.

He opened the box's flaps. And there it was: his book. *His book*. Dan swallowed. He allowed himself a moment of pride, and then he lined all fifty books on a shelf, where he could look at the whole row while he sat at his desk, and a whole row of eyes—the Cyclops colophon—looked right back at him, unblinking.

A reporter from the Lincoln *Journal* wrote a glowing review and interviewed Dan for the accompanying article. Dan credited conversations with "old friends"—Clare, Trent—as the inspiration for *Who's Your Demon?* Yes, he was excited that such a big press had published his book. Yes, he was glad to be back in Lincoln.

To celebrate the article, Dan and Jane met Trent and Betsy at the Legion Club for drinks. The Legion Club, a cavernous building on O Street, was billed as the World's Largest Post. Dan's parents went there when they wanted a "nice place" for special events. Dan and his friends slid into the same turquoise vinyl booths Dan had sat in as a child, sipping a Roy Rogers while his mother lifted a small, curvy glass that held her favorite drink, a King Alphonse.

The recollection of his childhood made him think, momentarily, of Clare's baby, the question of paternity. But then the waitress—an older woman who looked vaguely familiar—arrived with their drinks. She set the pitcher of beer on the table and squinted at Dan for a moment. "You were in the paper yesterday, weren't you? You wrote a book."

Dan nodded.

"Well," the waitress said, briskly, "then this pitcher's on the house. Enjoy!"

"Thank you," Dan said.

"Hey, man, you're a celebrity." Trent filled the glasses and handed them around.

Under the table, Jane's fingers pressed into his thigh. "You're like a rock star," she said.

"And we're your groupies," Betsy said. Everyone laughed; the old couples at the table next to them looked over and smiled; Dan raised his glass. He thought, *Lincoln is all I need. This is enough.*

Other times—like later that night, unable to sleep with the relentless wind he'd forgotten rattling the windows of his new house—he imagined the way his colleagues in Virginia would react to his celebrity. He could see their finely-chiseled features contorting, just slightly, in that East-coast academic wince at Dan's low-brow analysis, his pandering to the masses. And then Dan would think that Lincoln was all he deserved.

By the Saturday before Christmas, Dan's book filled the windows of local bookstores. Newspapers as far away as Los Angeles wrote reviews; not all glowing, of course—the *LA Times* called it "superficial but amusing"—but Dan couldn't complain about the amount of attention he'd received.

He was scheduled to give a signing at Nebraska Book at four o'clock. It was one of those winter days when the sun never appeared; by mid-afternoon, the sky had grown incrementally darker and a stiff wind blew relentlessly from the north. "Cold," Jane said as they walked toward the bookstore, her voice muffled by the scarf she'd wrapped around the lower half of her face, bandit-like.

"I know," Dan said. He figured the dreary weather would keep shoppers away, so he was startled when he stepped into the warmth of the store and looked toward the spiral staircase that led to the book department upstairs.

The staircase, coiled like a serpent, was packed with people who stood clutching copies of Dan's book against their chests.

"My God," Jane said.

Dan mounted the steps. He said, "Excuse me—I'm sorry—excuse me—" Jane followed, her fingers lightly around his elbow. Christmas music played over the speakers.

The men and women—mostly women—gave Dan shy, reverential smiles as he passed. Dan was near the top of the stairs when a woman reached out and clutched his gloved hand. "I just want you to know," she said, "how much *Who's Your Demon?* meant to me." Her fingers squeezed his, hard. Her gaze met Dan's. She had gray hair and dark, glittery eyes. "The chapter on Hamlet and the Deadly Sin of despair really *spoke* to me." She drew a breath and continued. "Your book saved my life."

Saved my life. Surely she was exaggerating. Still, Dan experienced a rush of some unnamable emotion in his chest, a sort of explosion—of triumph, or dread? What should he say? Jane's fingers dug into his elbow, like a tourniquet, and Dan didn't know if she was awestruck by his book's power, or giving him a warning.

"Thank you," he murmured to the woman. "I'm so glad to know you found it—helpful." She smiled, released his hand, and he and Jane continued up the stairs.

On Monday, Dan sat in his office, filling out the final grade sheets. Mary Phillmore called from New York City, to wish him a Merry Christmas and let him know that Cyclops was planning a big second printing of *Who's Your Demon?*

"You've sold fifty thousand copies as of December 15," Mary Phillmore said. "I think you tapped into the holiday gift market."

A second printing! Dan stared out the window, thinking how happy he should be, but behind his pleasure at the news sat a small, gnawing feeling of dread, as if there were a project he'd forgotten to do, or a looming deadline, or an unpaid debt.

Christmas Eve, Dan and Jane walked to Stratford Avenue, where everyone in the neighborhood gathered. They stood on sidewalks lined with votive candles in paper sacks, listened to Christmas carols ringing from loudspeakers attached to light posts, and admired decorative lights swirled through the pine trees and gleaming among the bare branches of oaks.

Once, in Virginia, Dan had criticized the Stratford Avenue Christmas fest. He'd called it tacky, overdone.

It was a beautiful evening. In Virginia, people would be shivering, bundled in their heaviest coats, complaining of cold; but for December in Nebraska, the air felt temperate. The snow that had fallen on Thanksgiving had mostly melted, except for piles that lined the curbs. The air smelled damp and clean.

Dan and Jane held hands as they walked. When they passed under streetlights, he saw the cold air had made her cheeks rosy. They turned onto Stratford and fell in behind a line of pedestrians strolling along the sidewalk. In the street, cars rolled slowly past, passengers' faces turning toward the windows, their gloved fingers pointing. *Look! Look!*

Dan greeted Gina and her two sons; Trent and Betsy waved from the cab of his pickup truck.

"It's all so pretty," Jane said.

And then Dan saw a couple pushing a stroller toward them. It could be anyone, he told himself, but the internal lurch of instinct said, *It's Clare.*

And it was Clare. Clare and her husband, the baby Emma in the stroller.

Dan raised his hand. His throat constricted with an emotion he couldn't identify. He made himself sound casual, surprised. "Clare! I didn't expect to run into you."

"Home for the holidays," Clare said. She looked—older, Dan thought. A little tired. In the heavy parka she wore, her body appeared thick. But she smiled at him, pleasantly, and said, "I'd like you to meet my husband, Desmond. This is Danny, an old friend from high school."

Desmond was tall, slightly stoop-shouldered, with thick blond hair. "Good to meet you," he said and offered his hand to Dan. *Old friend.* It was funny, wasn't it, that she'd chosen the same phrasing Dan had used in his Lincoln *Journal* interview, when he'd talked about the inspiration behind *Who's Your Demon?* Had she seen the article?

Dan introduced Jane. All the time, he forced himself not to stare too openly at the baby. He'd deluded himself when he believed he'd made peace with not-knowing; now he found himself consumed with curiosity. Mine or not mine? If he saw the baby up close, would he be able to tell?

"And this—" Clare leaned down and extracted the baby from her stroller— "is our daughter, Emma." Her hands clutched firmly against the baby's torso; Dan could tell the child was heavy. Solid. She was dressed in a fuzzy white outfit, a snowman embroidered on the front.

"Oh, she's darling," Jane said. "Can I hold her?"

Clare released Emma into Jane's arms and there she was, inches from Dan. She wore an alert, slightly suspicious expression. He couldn't tell what color her eyes were. Gray? Blue? Her nose was small and puggish—a typical baby's nose. Strands of dark hair curled around her face. Clare's hair was light brown, her husband's blond, Dan's own hair dark but straight. Where did Emma get her hair?

"Hey," Dan said. Emma looked at him. She cocked her head, reached out, and deliberately clutched her fingers in his scarf. She grinned.

He wanted to take it off, give it to her. His heartbeat slowed.

Clare said, "She's real interested in other people's things. A regular little Miss Covetousness."

"One of the Deadly Sins!" Jane said. "Have you read Dan's book?"

He should give Clare a copy, Dan thought. She'd probably be amused to see how the conversation on Halloween had inspired him—how he'd turned their little exchange into a book that had actually saved a person's life. *Saved a person's life.* What would she think about that? But then Emma tugged on his scarf, hard, and he looked at her dark eyes. Little Miss Covetousness. Wasn't there something about the Deadly Sin of covetousness he should remember? Was Clare sending him a clue? Was the baby his? He gazed at Clare; he willed her to meet his eyes, to let him know one way or the other. Faustus had said to Mephistopheles, *Sweet Devil, tell me—*.

But Clare was looking at Jane, shaking her head. *I will not.* "No," she said. "Not yet."

Emma made a little sound. Of discontent? Or disbelief? Dan wondered. As if she understood language and was offering her opinion. Frank Sinatra sang over the loudspeaker: *On the seventh day of Christmas, my true love gave to me—*.

"She's precious," Jane said. "You must be very happy."

Clare's husband hummed along with the carol: *Seven pipers piping, six geese a-laying, five gol-den rings—*. Cars passed, their exhaust pluming and dissipating in the cool air. The candles' flames swayed inside their sacks. When Jane handed the baby back to Clare, Emma was still holding Dan's scarf. He looked down and touched the baby's hand. The swath of cloth stretched out, linking the two of them for a moment before Emma flexed her fingers open and let it go.

Sitting Bull's Translator Remembers
the Speech in Bismarck, N.D.

The Northern Pacific was finally finished: all the spikes pounded in the ground, ties laid, smell of creosote uniting the town of Carleton, Minnesota, to the Washington Territory. Like a rain dance, the locomotive passing through the arid Plains would stimulate the formation of storm clouds—there was "scientific evidence," it was said—a story handed off from the Northern Pacific bond sellers to buyers and settlers. How could anyone argue that the railroad was an evil thing?

Of course the Indians did. They called it the Iron Horse, thought it brought bad luck, what with the wheel sparks flaring fires along its path, the noise scaring game away. Men rode the train to shoot buffalo from the windows and left the hulking carcasses to rot. From a distance, the dead beasts looked like hills of earth, small replicas of *Paha Sepa,* where the gold was found that led Custer into all his troubles. The railroad tracks made solid and visible the route of Lewis and Clark, a path anyone could follow, now.

The Northern Pacific finished! That called for celebration, a parade and speeches. This was long enough after Little Bighorn and the death of Custer—*Pehin Hanska*— that some forgiveness had been effected. Sitting Bull, the *wasicun* thought, had been tamed, a pet. He should be present at the railroad's dedication, everyone agreed. He could lead the parade through town, then be the first to speak.

I knew Lakota from my Army days, so I was sent to Standing

41

Rock to meet with the old chief. We decided this: he'd deliver his entire speech in Lakota, and when he'd finished, I would translate what he'd said. He'd talk of progress. He'd say he'd grown to understand the necessity of putting land to use. What an accomplishment, he would tell the audience, what a fine example of their perseverance. We stood outside his teepee when we planned this. It was the end of August, and light slanted in a way you never saw in the height of summer, green being leached from grass by drought and coming fall. The earth knew the season was changing, though you couldn't necessarily feel it in the air.

We might have shaken hands. It doesn't matter now.

The day of the parade we marched the main street of Bismarck. Dust rose around the horses' hooves; fields on the edge of the town were golden in the light. The sky hung blue as a plate overhead, strewn with clouds so high and white they could hardly be seen. A breeze lapped at the hems of ladies' skirts, twisting their hat ribbons like streamers.

When Sitting Bull stepped onto the wooden platform, how the *wasicun* applauded! The old Indian grinned. He held the reins of the show horse he'd been given by Buffalo Bill Cody, an animal white as a ghost, its tail, too, teased by the wind. The horse had been trained to dip to sitting when a gun was fired. Five years after the speech in Bismarck, the beast witnessed his master's death at Standing Rock. When Sitting Bull was shot, I've heard, the horse responded to the gunfire by beginning its routine. It knelt and rose in the steps of the Ghost Dance as if trying to raise the dead.

You say my facts aren't straight, that the horse came later? Well, you may be right; I may have conflated this meeting with another. Still, that's how I remember the afternoon in Bismarck. And hear me out—you'll know the end rings true.

Sitting Bull began his speech, and I knew I was in some trouble: He didn't say what we'd agreed. His words were *his*. I—the only other person there who knew Lakota—wondered if he meant this new speech to be a joke we shared.

The audience smiled back into his smiling face. He told a story none of them could comprehend, but when he chuckled, they chuckled in return. He raised one arm. A few in the audience raised their own. In the distance, I heard noise: a chuffing sound, the growing thunder of buffalo stampeding. Along the horizon, shapes that called to mind smoke signals trembled in the air. One lady turned, nervous. She must have thought the past was coming back.

But no: it was merely the train.

Sitting Bull continued. He never mentioned progress. He said that the love of possessions was like a disease with them, and the land upon which the railroad sat had been stolen from his tribe. They applauded, rising up like flames in the middle of the broken golden weeds. Still grinning—but only with his lips, I could see the anger in his eyes—he told the *wasicun*, "I hate you white devils," and I don't know what they thought he said, but the whole audience, as if one, tore off their hats, waved them wildly, and roared approval just as the train's conductor pulled his shrieking whistle and the whole landscape exploded with their noise.

Constellations

T he night before high school graduation, Abby and her
boyfriend Randy lay on the damp grass of Antelope Park,
resting their heads on a bright metal strip of railroad track,
and stared up at stars.

"There?" Randy said, pointing. "That's the Big Dipper, see?"

"Yes." Abby raised herself for a drink of Purple Passion from
the cup she and Randy were sharing. Her fingers felt sticky from
dipping the cup into the garbage can of Kool-Aid and Everclear
for refills. The designs of the constellations—some calculated,
some arbitrary—resembled the various groupings Abby could see
when she sat up: clusters of other graduating seniors made what
she supposed from the sky would look like significant
arrangements on the grass.

"The man in the moon," Randy said. "Looking down on us."
His nickname was Rabid, in acknowledgment of his tenacious
tackling ability on the football field. He was Abby's first serious
boyfriend, the first boy she'd slept with, and lying there on the
grass, both of them drunk, the hard metal pressing into the back of
her skull, their sticky hands touching, she experienced an odd kind
of comfort.

"I could never see him," Abby admitted.

The moon that night wasn't quite full, but Rabid said the face
appeared clearly visible. He began explaining the features to Abby.

"There's his mouth, right there? Think of the head being tilted a little. The mouth is sort of open, now can you see?"

"Kind of."

Why were they lying with their heads on the railroad tracks? It made perfect sense when they decided to do it—they wanted to look at the stars, and the best way seemed to be from a horizontal position, so you could take in the big picture, the whole sky hanging above you. The raised metal of the tracks offered the logical place to put their heads, like pillows.

"And those are his eyes, up near the top."

For a moment, Abby saw the face. "Yes." She turned to look at Rabid. The smell of creosote and damp grass surrounded them. Voices rose from the groups. Flames snapped and sparked from the fire in the grill next to the picnic tables. Rabid's eyelids twitched and then closed.

"You can see him," he said. He smiled, already drifting off, and Abby smiled back—even though she knew he couldn't see—and shut her eyes, too.

What happened next was never entirely clear. They'd both fallen asleep or passed out. Abby knew that much. Someone had dragged one of the picnic tables close to the tracks, and Abby's best friend, Teresa, was stretched out on one of the seats. Asleep, or passed out. The garbage can—the punch bucket—lay tipped on its side, also near the tracks, indicating that the party had orbited closer to where Abby and Rabid lay. As if their friends had moved in to keep them company while they slept. All of these details sank into Abby's consciousness the second she opened her eyes, roused by—what? Roused by Rabid's hand on her arm, urgent.

"Ab, get up, the train's coming."

Air slammed into Abby's lungs when she inhaled. She leapt to her feet and stumbled a few feet away from the tracks. She and Rabid stood clutching each other, breathing heavily through their dry mouths. Abby's head hammered, the beginning of a hangover.

A few moments passed in silence. Abby began to doubt Rabid,

and then she heard, in the distance, the low whine of the train's whistle. Almost instantly, the clack of wheels along the tracks grew louder, the ground under her feet vibrating from the tons of weight hurtling toward where they'd been lying.

Sparks sprang from the train's wheels, which made a rhythmic noise, like a record player's needle circling at the end of the album. The force of the passing train tugged their hair and clothes in its wake. On the picnic bench, Teresa slept on, oblivious. She was almost as close to the train as Abby and Rabid had been, and she didn't hear a thing.

"How did you know?" Abby whispered to Rabid. She hadn't yet become fully conscious of the fact they could have died.

"It was like a sign," Rabid said. His face wore the shocked expression of a man who'd been confronted with a space alien or live dinosaur, something that defied all his firmly held beliefs. "I just—I just knew. It came to me, that I should wake up and move. It was a sign."

The next day, no one believed Rabid. They offered other explanations—that he'd felt vibrations, that he'd woken up naturally, that someone else had woken him up and he'd forgotten about it. Teresa claimed that the train *couldn't* have passed without her being aware of it. Abby turned out to be the only one who thought Rabid had told the truth. She liked the notion of signs, signals, the idea that Rabid had somehow been chosen. That there had been a reason for them to live.

Twenty years later, early morning, Abby stood over the kitchen table, glancing at the newspaper while she waited for the boys to finish getting ready for school. Her husband, Tim, had left for work moments earlier, swinging the case of pharmaceutical samples he would hand out to doctors around town, smacking a quick kiss against her check. A pile of expired tetracycline samples in stiff plastic wrappers sat next to the sink, waiting for Abby to responsibly grind them up in the disposal. Abby skimmed the headlines, then turned to the Public Record to see if anyone she knew had had a baby or was getting divorced. The Obituaries faced the Public Record, and Abby was in the process of closing the paper when she saw Rabid's name.

> Lang, Randall, 38, Washington, DC. Formerly of Lincoln, graduate of Lincoln Southeast, American University. Victim of pedestrian-automobile accident in Washington on 4-30. Services pending. Survived by parents, Mr. and Mrs. Walter Lang, Lincoln; sister, Mary Beth Koening, Fremont; two nieces. Memorials may be sent to charity of donor's choice.

Rabid. Abby felt short of breath, on the verge of hyperventilating. Rabid, dead! She became conscious of the pose she'd struck—mouth open, one hand over her heart. As if she'd maintained secret, strong feelings for him all these years, feelings that the news of his death brought hurtling to the surface.

They'd broken up, amicably enough, at the end of the summer before college. He was going off to school, all the way to Washington, D.C.; she was staying in Lincoln. He'd gotten a job in D.C. after he graduated. For a little while, a rumor circulated that he was working for the CIA, but then she heard it was at a more normal place, like the Department of the Interior. Or was it the State Department? And he'd been married, though apparently it hadn't lasted, since no surviving spouse was listed in the obituary.

What had his daily life been like? She couldn't imagine, and now there was no possibility of finding out.

"My God," Abby whispered, still staring at the newspaper. She couldn't decide what to do next. She wanted a cigarette, though she almost never smoked. She wanted to talk to Teresa, her best friend since even before she'd known Rabid. What she wanted most, though, she admitted to herself, was a drink.

"Boys!" Abby called. She picked up her purse. "Don't want to be late to school!" Their feet pounded against the stairs. Davey appeared in the kitchen first, Jason lagging a few steps behind. Davey grinned. He was seven, the older brother by a year, and his top front teeth had fallen out, giving his smile an impoverished, unfinished look. Abby focused on the gap at the front of his mouth, his bright pink gums, to distract herself. In rehab, they told you to repeat the word *stop* in your head, over and over, when the craving for a drink hit.

Stop. Stop.

She drove the boys to school. They kissed her and clambered out of the back seat. *Stop*, Abby told herself, even as she steered the car toward South Street. She followed Seventeenth to N, where she turned into the parking lot of N Street Drive Inn and went inside the big, anonymous liquor store miles from her house. Rabid had bought the Everclear for their pre-graduation party here, using a driver's license that belonged to his sister's boyfriend. And then they'd driven to the Hinky Dinky on O Street for packages of Kool-Aid. Rabid also bought bottles of grape juice to doctor up the Purple Passion a bit, an idea that had seemed exotic and sophisticated. Abby smiled to herself, selecting a bottle of the Chardonnay she liked from the cooler.

Carrying the wine back to the car, Abby found that the feeling of anxiety, the feeling of guilt, had gone away. How easy it was to backslide!

In her four weeks of sobriety, Abby didn't think about drinking all the time. She didn't find herself sitting at stoplights, fantasizing about gin and tonics or cold cans of beer. Sober was sober. It was a flat line on an EKG, steady. It wasn't the drinks she missed so much as the experience of being drunk, receiving those flashes of

insight inspired by three or four beers, the way she became
incredibly conscious of smells—the scent of burning leaves
contained the whole tragic yet invigorating experience of
shortening, chilly days—and the sad dying light of the sun on winter
afternoons. Connections she'd never noticed before descended
into her field of vision: Birds in the grass, grass pulled for nests,
dead grass enclosing the eggs of growing baby birds. Everything
in the world touching every other thing!

At home, she slipped the bottle out of its protective sack and
set it on the top shelf of the refrigerator. The watercolor pastels
on the label suggested an indistinct but benevolent landscape.
Mondriano Chardonnay. The wine was tinged faintly with a pastel
color of its own, golden behind the glass container. Abby shut the
refrigerator. She pressed both hands against the door and waited
for her better instincts to take over and make her grab the bottle,
pour the wine down the sink, and repent. She waited for this to
happen, and when it didn't, she went upstairs to take a shower.

She turned on the water and adjusted the temperature. The
shower curtain's hooks rattled against the rod when she stepped
into the tub. Under the warm spray, Abby turned, trying to focus
only on water, not on the bottle of wine, or the fact of Rabid,
dead.

In the weeklong, overnight rehab program in Omaha, you were
supposed to tell what brought you there—a judge's orders after
the police wrote up a citation for leaving your children in a locked
car while you went into a bar for five hours; or losing a job; or a
confrontation between you and your family, where they turned on
you in the name of *tough love*. People told their stories and wept,
even the men, their mouths contorted, grief seeming to alter the
color of their skin. Abby felt terrible during these episodes. She
wished she'd been the sort of person who'd reach out and whisper,
"It's okay," instead of looking away, relieved that she'd bummed

a cigarette earlier and could busy herself with exhaling smoke and tapping ashes against the side of an ashtray.

One of the problems with rehab—and there were a number of problems, not the least being Abby's angry and animated roommate, Donna—was that Abby herself didn't *have* an incident that compared with any of the confessions she heard. The stories she had about drinking were funny stories, or the night Rabid received his sign as they lay on the railroad tracks, and no one ever believed that one anyway. As the week wore on, she understood that the other members of the group were beginning to regard her as snotty or resistant. But that wasn't fair—what was she supposed to do, make something up? So she finally told them the worst story connected to drinking that she knew, even though she'd only been a witness to, not a participant in, what happened. The story hadn't gotten the response she'd hoped for, and she understood now—as she stood forcefully scouring the bar of soap with a washcloth, working up lather—that this was due to the story's ambiguity.

A Friday night, late fall, her sophomore year of college. The Phi Delts were throwing a party in one of the big fields a few miles beyond the outskirts of town. The party was like other parties Abby and Teresa had gone to that fall: bracing night air, beer icy cold in plastic cups, a bonfire crackling and sending up sparks. She and Teresa leaned together, laughing. Stars salted the dark sky. No moon. It was hard to see anyone unless you were standing right next to the fire or huddled close around the keg.

And then—Jesus, Abby could still see it, telling the story in rehab, and now in the shower, shampoo trailing down the sides of her face, eyes squeezed shut, one hand against the tile wall for balance. Even now, her heart caught in her throat.

She and Teresa had gone into a stand of trees on the far side of the field to pee. That's what saved them: they had to go to the bathroom. They walked back toward the bonfire, congratulating themselves on their foresight for stuffing little packages of Kleenex in their purses to use as toilet paper. "That's *so good* we remembered," Abby said. She thought her speech sounded a little slurred, so she tried again. "That is *so* good we remembered."

They were fifty yards from the bonfire, which was in a hollow made by the downward slope of a tiny hill. Abby looked toward the fire. Its brightness seemed unusually intense, almost holy, a halo glowing around the flames. She heard a mechanical noise which grew louder as she listened. Light hovered along the ridge of the hill, illuminating figures. Headlights, she realized. *A car!*

Someone was driving across the rutted field. The engine paused, then whined with effort. Later she learned that the tires had been stuck in the sandy soil, and the driver punched the accelerator to get some traction. Figures by the fire turned toward the noise. The car erupted suddenly over the top of the hill. People on the outskirts of the fire ran. Some of the girls were screaming.

But two students didn't get out of the way in time. One was a Phi Delt, a junior, and the other was a girl from one of the sororities down by the railroad tracks. A Phi Mu? All these years later, Abby couldn't quite remember, though at the time the accident had given the sorority a sudden deluge of attention. The sheen of tragedy, a certain distinction.

The car's nose pushed their bodies up over the hood. The boy and girl fell on opposite sides of the vehicle, which finally jerked to a halt a few feet from the bonfire. In the horrible silence, Abby heard the boy who'd been hit yelling. The driver climbed out of the car, took a step, and collapsed.

Tim Weaver moved into the firelight. He was a senior, pre-med then, the MCAT that forced him to reconsider his plans yet unscored. Abby had never seen him before. He ordered someone to get a hold of an ambulance, knelt and pressed his fingers against the fallen girl's throat, kept the Phi Delt from trying to stand. What he did had no effect on the ultimate outcome—the girl and boy both died. But he was the first to move toward them, away from his own helpless horror, the first person to *do something*.

Plastic cups melted against the ground around the fire. Watching Tim, Abby understood, as clearly as if someone had whispered in her ear, that here was the sort of boy a girl would be smart to marry. She dropped her cup of beer into the weeds and walked toward him to see if she could help.

Abby stepped out of the shower, dried off, and pulled on one of Tim's old sweatshirts and a pair of jeans. The people in rehab liked stories with a clear-cut moral, not ones like Abby's story where the horror of the accident balanced against the fact that the accident was the reason she met her husband. And meeting Tim had structured the rest of her life in a certain pleasant, comfortable way. An enviable way.

She carefully stroked blush on her cheeks, conscious of how she wasn't rushing downstairs and ripping open the refrigerator door to lift the chilled bottle of wine to her lips and guzzle. No, she had no reason to hurry. The hours ahead—and it was only ten o'clock, early—hovered before her with the same pastel benevolence of the wine bottle's label. She dried her hair, checked her appearance in the bathroom mirror, considered and decided against earrings. Then she went downstairs.

She took a wineglass out of the cupboard. From the window above the sink, she could see a plane bisecting the sky, too far away to hear. She wondered if Rabid would be buried here in Lincoln, if that particular plane might be transporting his coffin in its cargo hold. She opened the refrigerator. Against her fingers, the bottle felt perfectly chilled. She filled the glass with wine, placed it on the table, and settled into a chair. She waited, giving herself one more chance to change her mind.

Condensation formed on the glass. Abby's hand reached out. Her fingers touched the moisture. Slick, cold. She lifted the glass. She closed her eyes. She drank. The taste of fruit bloomed in her mouth, small distinct sparks of flavor exploding against her tongue.

When she opened her eyes, the white kitchen walls seemed to glow, tinted faintly with pink.

Abby thought again that she might like a cigarette, though really she wasn't much of a smoker, not like those people in rehab. Jesus, the air in the rooms where they gathered to tell their stories was actually *thick*, worse than the air in any bar Abby'd gone to. She'd bummed a few cigarettes while she was there, but only because smoking was something to do while you listened. For a week, she sat in a room with the same five people, and they talked and talked and talked. Endless drone of voices, scraps of pop psychology, pep talks and forced intimacy. The price she'd had to pay for Tim catching her and Teresa drunk in the middle of the day.

Maybe she should have told the story in rehab of how she'd gotten there, but it was a boring story, Abby thought, finishing the wine and letting the glass sit for a moment on the table before she filled it again. A boring story, and it only revealed how different she was from the other people there, how her problem wasn't that *she* had a problem, but that her husband thought she did.

On the day Jason and Teresa's youngest girl both started all-day kindergarten this past fall, Teresa showed up for lunch with a bottle of white wine. Wasn't finally having all their kids in school cause for celebration? she'd joked. Abby fixed salads. That first day, they mixed the wine with club soda ("Isn't that how you make a wine spritzer?"), but it tasted awful, fizzy and watered down. They laughed about Ladies' Lunch, and that first one was so much fun they decided to make it a weekly event. A set of unarticulated rules evolved: they never drank more than the single bottle of wine, though sometimes it was one of those big bottles (a magnum? Was that the term?) and they always finished it by one thirty, to give themselves time to sober up before the kids got home from school. They'd each have two cups of strong black coffee, then drive around Lincoln looking for the right place to dispose of the empty wine bottle. Of course they couldn't just toss it in Abby's garbage for anyone to discover. Hiding the bottle was part of the fun of Ladies' Lunch, the way a certain anonymous trash bin would present itself and become a co-conspirator in their secret.

The last Ladies' Lunch, the day Tim caught them, took place in March. Abby drove down 10th Street, cautious, obeying the speed limit, checking in her rear-view mirror. In the passenger seat, Teresa lit a cigarette, even though she'd officially quit. "We'd better stop and get some Lysol or something," she said. "I don't want to stink up your car."

Abby pulled into the U Stop across the street from the City County Building. A chilly wind made the metal signs with the gas prices shudder and rattle. Teresa smoked her cigarette while Abby hustled inside to buy a can of Lysol.

"That all?" inquired the clerk. "Need anything else? Cigarettes? Maybe it's your lucky day, you want to take a chance with a couple pickle cards?"

Abby laughed. Later she'd wonder why he asked. Was she acting drunk, on the verge of a shopping spree, agreeing to purchase anything he mentioned? At the time it seemed harmless and funny, especially the term *pickle cards*. "That's all," she said.

Outside, she handed the Lysol to Teresa, who, in exchange, handed Abby the empty wine bottle they needed to throw away. "There's a Dumpster over there," she said, pointing.

"Perfect."

Teresa got out of the car, took a last drag, and dropped the cigarette on the ground. Sparking, the butt skittered toward the gas pumps, and Teresa chased after it, laughing. "Go!" Abby yelled, holding up the bottle, cheering Teresa on. "Go!" This was the moment Tim must have driven by, on his way to meet a group of dermatologists for a late lunch at Lazlo's, and had seen them.

There you go, Abby imagined telling the group at rehab. She raised her glass in a toast as if the group were in the room with her, sitting around the kitchen table. *That's my story, that's how I got here. Ladies' Lunch.*

There'd been a confrontation that evening with Tim, but a fairly mild confrontation. Abby had put the boys to bed and was straightening up the kitchen, nursing a Bud Light, when Tim said, "We need to talk." He stood in front of the open refrigerator door with his back to her.

"All right," Abby said. The beginning of a headache tapped behind her eyes, so she took one of the Pfizer sample packages of ibuprofen from the cupboard above the sink and pried at the foil back. "Here?"

"Oh, let's go in the living room." There was something about his tone she didn't like—a forced joviality, a suspicious sense of camaraderie. He held a can of diet Coke in one hand. Abby picked up her beer and followed him out of the kitchen.

In the living room, he sat on the couch and patted the cushion next to him. Since the beginning of their marriage, there had been a slow, downhill slide on the amount of time they spent together— it happened to everyone, Abby knew from talking to Teresa. All the things needing to be done that required their separate attentions: the dishes in the kitchen that Abby wanted to get loaded in the dishwasher, the game on television in the den that Tim should watch with the boys. Now, it felt strange to be sitting in the living room alone with him because it had been such a long time since they'd done it.

Abby took a drink of her beer. Tim reached over and removed the can from her hand. He set it on the table and closed his fingers around hers. "Abby, I think you need to check into a rehab center in Omaha and get your drinking under control. I made a couple of calls today, and the Med Center has this weeklong program—it would be sort of a little vacation for you—"

"What are you talking about?" Abby's fingers twitched, involuntarily. "What do you mean, get my drinking under control?"

"At parties, sometimes, you just get sort of, sort of *loud*," Tim said. He looked away. He didn't like saying these things; he was forcing himself, she could tell.

"Like when?"

"Like last Sunday when we went over to watch football with the Dreisers. And two weeks ago at that Pfizer cocktail party down at the Cornhusker."

Abby frowned. She remembered both events clearly—she'd had a few drinks, had a good time. *Loud.* She didn't remember being *loud.*

"And then this afternoon, I saw you and Teresa at that U Stop on 10th Street—"

"What?"

"I was driving down to Lazlo's. You were stumbling around the parking lot, holding a bottle—"

"I was not stumbling," Abby said. "I was not."

"You were," Tim said. "And Teresa was smoking, I thought she'd quit." He raised one hand, to keep her from saying anything else. "I know you've got a lot on your plate." He was trying to be reasonable, persuasive, empathetic—as if he'd read an article on the best way to approach *an alcoholic.* "The boys, taking care of the house, a lot of responsibility, but sometimes it probably gets pretty monotonous for you, too."

Abby shrugged. She folded her arms across her chest.

"But it seems to me like there's beginning to be a problem— I'm not saying there *is* one—"

"If you think I need to stop drinking, I'll stop. There's no reason to go into, into *rehab.* Jesus."

Tim regarded her patiently. "From what I've read, the chances of success are so much higher when there's a—structured program. And experts involved."

Structured program. Experts involved. Doctor's rhetoric—as if he'd actually managed to make it into medical school and were speaking to a patient, rather than his wife.

"I'd just hate for things to get to the point where I'm worrying about the boys—"

The appeal to her motherly instincts! "I'd *never* hurt the boys."

"I know." Tim tilted his face away from her for a moment, and Abby realized he was on the verge of tears.

She must have been drunk then, letting his show of emotion move her beyond reason. *So, what's one week, maybe it* will *be like a vacation.* She lifted the beer to her mouth. The can was almost empty, and, although she didn't know it then, it was the last drink she would have for four weeks.

Tim didn't believe the story about Rabid receiving his sign, which Abby related a few weeks after they'd started dating. But he told her about the third rail, a piece of electrified track that ran between the normal lines of track. If you touched the third rail, you would be instantly electrocuted. "Wow," Abby had said. They were lingering over dinner at Pontillo's, pizza crusts piled on their plates. Had there been a third rail in Antelope Park, another danger that night that she and Rabid had successfully avoided?

Tim knew about the third rail because his grandfather had been an engineer on the Union Pacific that ran between Norfolk and Lincoln. A true engineer, with the striped overalls and hat, a red bandanna tucked in his pocket. Tim's grandfather had run his train for years, until an incident happened to a friend who engineered the train that ran east to west across Nebraska. One late night, near Alliance, the friend turned his attention away for just a second—to rub his eyes or something, Tim said. When he looked back, a girl had appeared in the headlight, walking down the center of the tracks, right in the train's path. Of course the engineer slammed on the brakes, but the girl must have known how long it took a train to stop. "Granddad heard later she'd been pregnant, the guy wouldn't marry her, and she decided to end it," Tim finished. "And Granddad figured it was time to retire before something like that turned up in front of *his* train."

What an awful story, Abby thought, retrieving the wine bottle. She decided to leave it on the table to save trips back and forth from the refrigerator. She imagined the engineer's shock when the girl glowed suddenly in front of him, then the horrible shriek of brakes, followed by a thump. All the time, the whistle blaring its warning.

Back in high school, Rabid told her he always listened for the train's whistle before he went to sleep. They waited for it together one night when his parents were out of town and Abby lied to her own parents, saying she was sleeping over at Teresa's. It was winter, she remembered, cold enough to make frost ferns bloom in the corners of the windows. She and Rabid lay pressed together on his single bed, astonished by the comfort of sex on a mattress rather than in the crowded confines of his old Satellite.

"It always comes through about midnight," Rabid said. "And then again at three, at least sometimes. I don't always hear that one."

"Three is late," Abby murmured. She drifted off to sleep, listening.

At rehab, after she'd finished her story about the accident, one of the men in the group, Tony, nodded. He was the one she usually bummed cigarettes from. "I remember that, it was in the paper."

"Did they die right there in the field?" Donna, her roommate, chewed her thumb and stared at Abby.

"I think it was later, in the ambulance or after they'd gotten to the hospital."

Donna glared at her, as if Abby were supposed to remember better. "What happened to the guy who was driving the car?"

Abby bit her lower lip. "I don't think he was hurt. Physically, I mean. He was from somewhere else, visiting a friend for the weekend. I think. It's been a long time."

"So what does it have to do with you?"

Abby sighed. She understood Donna's dislike was rooted in the contrast between Donna's stringy blonde hair and chewed cuticles and Abby's bangs, artfully highlighted to cover the gray, her painted nails. Abby had a husband employed by a big pharmaceutical company; Donna was a single mother. The only thing that Donna held over Abby was that Donna's sufferings had been greater, that she understood more fully the depth of sorrow in the world.

"I was there," Abby said. "I saw it, that's all."

"That's enough, isn't it?" Tony asked. "Seeing?"

"Why are you even *here*?" Donna asked Abby. "Are you a *newspaper reporter* or something? Are you just here to watch the rest of us who really know what it's like?"

The rest of the group stared down at their hands. Did they agree with Donna, that Abby was some sort of dilettante? Christ. The muscles in Abby's face tightened. She'd tried: she'd made the lists they were supposed to make, drank the burned-tasting coffee served in the TV room after supper, sat through these endless sessions with people she knew she'd never see again. She'd told the story about that horrible night, which had stayed with her for years. And now no one would look at her. Abby slid a cigarette out of Tony's pack and lit it. Two days left, she thought. And for the next two days she was mute, not responding to Donna's "Good night," nodding if someone spoke to her, sometimes smiling, but not uttering another word until Tim came to pick her up.

She stepped out of the front door of the clinic. Salt speckled the walk; there'd been an ice storm earlier that morning. The air smelled wet and cold. Behind her, she heard Donna and Tony making plans to attend an AA meeting. Tim smiled at her, holding out his arms for a hug.

"How are you doing?" he asked.

"Fine," Abby said. She met Tim's eyes. He was trying to see, she could tell, if she'd been transformed.

❧

Abby poured the last drizzle of wine into her glass. Maybe Donna's point had been that Abby *wasn't* an alcoholic, because she didn't have one of those true, brutal stories to share. In Donna's mind, Abby'd had no reason to be at rehab, and Abby found herself nodding in agreement. "Right on," Abby said to an imaginary Donna.

When she glanced at the clock on the stove, she was startled to see it was almost two, a little later than she expected. She stood, holding on to the back of her chair, and then made a pot of coffee. She felt—she felt fairly drunk, she admitted to herself. It would be safer, she decided, to walk to meet the boys. They lived only seven or eight blocks from Sheridan Elementary; it was a nice afternoon; the walk would do her good. They could stop by Leon's for an after-school snack. And then, on the way home, she would visit the railroad tracks in a tribute to Rabid.

"All right," Abby said. She moved around the kitchen, drinking her coffee, wrapping up the wine bottle in the morning's newspaper to hide in a garbage can somewhere. When she bumped her shin against the back of one of the chairs, she thought of a cartoon injury, how a string of stars indicated pain. She knew she'd have a bruise.

The expired tetracycline tablets were still sitting by the sink. Abby found a paper grocery bag and put the wine bottle and pills inside.

She slipped on her sunglasses and set off along the undulating sidewalk toward Sheridan. When she arrived at the school, the boys looked surprised to see her on foot. "Where's the car?" Jason asked. He was such a worrier, Abby thought. Just like his father.

"At home," Abby said. She had the grocery sack tucked firmly under her arm. "It's a nice day, I thought we'd stop at Leon's and get a snack."

"Is the car okay?" Jason asked.

"It's fine," Abby said.

"Are *you* okay?" Davey asked.

"Of course!" She smiled at him and, after a second, he smiled back.

"What's in the sack?"

"Just some garbage. Come on, let's go."

Outside Leon's, Abby handed Davey a ten and told him to get whatever they wanted. "I'm going to put this in the trash," she said, motioning with her head toward the incinerator that sat at the far corner of the parking lot. The incinerator was the size of a Dumpster, with an eternal fire going inside to burn pallets and broken-down boxes.

"All right," Davey said. She pretended he wasn't looking at her suspiciously.

She crossed the lot to the incinerator. There was a little open space, like a window, on one side. Abby aimed and tossed the sack. It sailed inside the incinerator, landing with a thud. A burst of flame flashed in the window and a horrible smell of cooked plastic wafted toward her.

"Here." Davey had appeared suddenly at her elbow, and was forcing things on her: change from the ten-dollar bill, a fudgcicle.

"Hold on," Abby said. She got the money into her pocket and began unwrapping the ice cream. A wisp of cold smoke wafted off the top of the fudgcicle, like exhaled breath on a cold day. She took a bite and walked toward a row of skinny pine trees that divided the grocery store's land from Antelope Park, the place where Rabid had received his sign. Abby pushed her way between two of the trees, raising a smell of juniper, branches grabbing at her hair.

"Where are we going?"

"I want to see something."

She took a deep breath. She made herself pay close attention to everything around her. The air against her cheeks lacked all traces of the hard wintery edge it held the day she left rehab. The scent of mud filled her nose. It was spring. Spring! Twenty years ago, there was an afternoon the air smelled like this, a weird warm day at the beginning of February. A false spring, because bitter cold returned two days later. But Abby and Rabid took advantage of the beautiful weather and drove out to Pioneers Park in his sister's convertible. The car's top was down, and a fifth of something clanked around under the seat. They took surreptitious sips—Bacardi, wasn't it?—the wind whipping Abby's hair around her face, Rabid laughing, his teeth glinting in the sun, the infinite and understanding sky above them. Was it because Rabid had been a little drunk that he'd looked at her and said *I love you*?

The first stunning time a boy had said those words. And now he was dead.

Abby crossed the space of grass to the railroad tracks and glanced down the gleaming strips of metal. There was no third rail. The tracks, as tracks went, appeared to be fairly safe.

"Well," she said. The fudgcicle was melting against her fingers. She took another bite and tossed the remainder into a trash can. With the boys following, she walked to the spot where she and Rabid had lain all those years ago to look at the constellations. The tracks seemed to be higher than she remembered. Gravel coated the rise leading up to them and covered the ground between the ties. She'd completely forgotten about the rocks. She sank to her knees and put her hand on the rail where Rabid's head must have been when he received the sign.

Rabid, dead. She had to keep reminding herself.

"Mommy?" Davey looked down at her, his eyes anxiously focused on hers. "Maybe we should go over by the swings? So a train doesn't hit us?"

"A train won't hit us," Abby said. She slid her legs along the ground and twisted her torso so she could rest her head against the rail. The gravel was so tightly packed it felt like a smooth surface, not uncomfortable at all. Above her, Abby saw the faces of her sons, watery blue sky rippling over their heads. She stretched out her arms and legs, like a child making an angel in snow, the way she and Rabid had positioned themselves. The five points of their bodies must have made the shape of two stars on the tracks.

She turned so that she lay with the smooth metal against her cheek, her ear pressed into it as if against a shell, and closed her eyes.

"What are you doing?" Jason's voice had the tone that meant Abby would need to use strenuous calming measures in a moment. In a moment. In a moment, Abby would raise her head from the tracks, take her sons' hands in her hands, and begin the walk toward home. But for now, she waited, positioned as Rabid had been, resting, all those years ago. This is how he must have received the sign.

"I'm listening for something."

"Listening for what?"

Was there the tiniest sound, not even a noise but a vibration? Was this what Rabid had heard; is this how he knew to save them? The fillings in Abby's back molars tingled as if picking up some errant radio station. She waited. She wanted more. The rail warmed against her skin. Her fingers were sticky from the melted fudgcicle. With the boys quiet, waiting for her answer, she could almost believe she'd turned back time to twenty years ago. If she turned her head and opened her eyes, Rabid would be lying next to her, both of them feeling the tingling in their molars—that secret of the train coming toward them—their mouths on the verge of filling with speech.

Who Watches Over Us

He was borne on a train from New York City: nine tons of bronze sculpted into a hooded man sowing grain by hand, designed and destined for the top of Nebraska's state capitol. From that vantage point, he would look down over the city of Lincoln. The folds of the hood shadowed his face. A pouch of grain hung across his chest. He held one strong arm poised to fling seeds the size of shotgun shells.

Arrived in Lincoln, he was left lying on the capitol's lawn as though dead, a mysterious artifact like those heads on Easter Island, carved and left by whom?

To raise him twenty stories to the building's top took planning. A crowd gathered in the streets to watch. Some folks spoke behind their hands: they didn't like his looks, that hood, the way his eyes were blank as stones. The sower marked the beginning of the growing cycle, yes, but who marked the end; who marked the harvest? Another hooded man they didn't want to name.

But others thought him noble, his eyes blind like Justice's, or indifferent like the weather that descended without provocation or favor. He was, they thought, of them.

From his prone position, he was pushed upright by men who grunted with the effort. Then a derrick hauled the sower in the air. The crowd watched him rise and rise. Suspended, he swayed from side to side, then ascended to the capitol's dome, the highest point in Lincoln.

So far from the ground, he looked not much bigger than a normal man, a mere mortal. Still, we feel him watching. At night, he's almost invisible against the dark sky, but we turn our eyes toward the light placed between his feet, which warns low-flying planes to stay away. The light is red. It blinks on and off in a rhythmic way, and the blameless among us think it looks like the beating heart of someone sleeping; we sinners see it pounding like the heart of something chased.

The Slave Trade

In February, Thedford Junior-Senior High held its annual Slave Auction. Emily Ambrose stood with other cheerleaders and the football players, waiting her turn on the auction block, which was really only a little platform at the back of the lunchroom. The air smelled of cooked food, Clorox, and mothballs. Most everyone in town came to the auction, even some ranchers from Senecca who didn't have any sons at home to help with the spring calving. They'd buy themselves a football player or two, sometimes a cheerleader who'd gotten herself a reputation as a hard worker.

The hem of Emily's cheerleading skirt chafed her legs. A big fan in the corner rustled the tissue streamers of pompoms she held, one pressed against each hipbone. Right now her cousin, Eddy Ambrose, stood on the block. Emily's friend Denise would follow Eddy, then Emily, and behind Emily were three of the biggest football players, the real money-makers.

Emily turned her head to make her hair slide back behind her shoulders. She kept her gaze away from the front row, where her parents sat. Eighteen years ago, her parents had been students at Thedford High, and had stood—as they used to remind her in dreamy, reminiscent voices—on the auction block themselves. Emily's mother had worn *her* cheerleader outfit; Emily's father, the star quarterback for the Thedford Tigers, dressed in his shoulder pads and helmet. They'd been the Homecoming Queen and King that fall. The yearbook was filled with their pictures. Along with the rest of their class, the two of them brought in so much money that almost a quarter of the books in the library contained little stickers printed with *Gift from the class of 1963*.

Now, her parents had been divorced for a little over a year. In the front row, three empty seats separated the two of them, even though all the other chairs in the room were taken and a few men leaned against the back wall. But who in their right mind would sit between Walter Ambrose and his ex-wife? Since *the incident*—Christmas Eve a year ago when her father lost his temper and swung a hammer at her mother's skull—Emily's days had been saturated with mortification, fed by her understanding that the whole town *knew*, that she herself was a figure of some curiosity, the blended molecules of a man who could lose his temper to that extent and the woman who bore a dramatic scar along the side of her face. A *Gothic* scar, Emily thought. Even from a distance, the jagged line looked like a country road delineated on a map.

"Do I hear seventy-five?" Dr. Donaldson hollered into a bullhorn. Eddy Ambrose stared down at his feet. Seventy-five was a respectable amount, like a B+ on a test that you'd be happy to admit to anyone, happy to remember later.

An old farmer sitting in back lifted one hand.

"Seventy-five it is. Do I hear eighty?"

No one responded. "All right, then," Dr. Donaldson said. "Eddy Ambrose, sold for seventy-five dollars to the gentleman in the back row." It was standard auction procedure for the purchased student to join the purchaser, for them to sit together and discuss what the master wanted the slave to do, so Eddy— smiling bashfully—made his way down the aisle.

Denise's boyfriend's parents bought her for fifty dollars. Emily guessed that Denise would be invited over to make dinner, an easy task, something that Denise would like to do anyway. Denise joined the Walkers in the audience. And then—Emily thought of the line in

Heart of Darkness: "The horror! The horror!"—her turn had arrived. She stepped next to Dr. Donaldson. She smiled at the crowd, toward the back of the room, over the heads of her parents.

"Emily Ambrose is head cheerleader, and I hear she makes a mean apple pie," Dr. Donaldson said. "Who wants to start? Who'll give me twenty?"

"Twenty," Emily's mother said.

"Thirty," her father countered.

"Forty," Emily's mother said. She didn't look at Emily's father. Holding her purse in her lap, she gazed placidly at Emily on the stage. At last year's auction, a bare six weeks after *the incident*, Emily's parents did this exact same thing, bidding against each other until her father gave up. Immediately after the auction, you were required to pay Dr. Donaldson, in cash, for the student you'd purchased. The year before, Emily's mother had bid two hundred dollars—almost all their grocery money for February— before her father dropped out.

"Fifty," Emily's father said. Around town, he'd recently been given the nickname of Boo, after Boo Radley in *To Kill a Mockingbird*, because Emily's father, like Boo, almost never came out of his house on the north edge of town. His nickname annoyed Emily, not because her father was undeserving of ridicule, but because Boo Radley had been a kind person, despite his peculiarities. He saved Scout and Jem from Bob Ewell's knife; he left little gifts for Scout in the trunk of the old tree.

Dr. Donaldson didn't even have to prompt her parents to keep the numbers rising in installments of ten. "Sixty," said Emily's mother. The rest of the audience watched in silence. Emily had grown used to the taste of humiliation, the bitter flavor of a chewed lemon peel that filled her mouth during times she knew people were looking at her and thinking about *the incident*. *The incident* had taken place a little over a year ago, and no one in Thedford had forgotten it. Oh, to move to a town where no one knew you! Lincoln—where she was planning on going to college next year—might not be far enough, Emily thought, waiting to hear her father's voice.

"Seventy," he said. She might need to move to a different state entirely.

The summer when Emily first noticed things going bad between her parents, five years ago, was the summer a new family moved into the house behind Emily's. The house had been vacant since its owner died in January, and Emily's father sometimes stood in the backyard, staring at it, talking to himself, but loudly enough that anyone in the vicinity could hear: "Oughta buy that place and turn it into a shop where I could have some space for my furniture work. Use the land for a garden, plant a bunch of tomatoes." But the purchase never materialized; the people who inherited the house didn't want to sell it. Instead, they rented the place out to a Pentecostal minister, his wife, and their two daughters.

The girls' names were Ruth and Sarah. Ruth was eleven, Emily's age, and Sarah was nine. They both had beautiful long hair that hung past their waists. "It's never been cut," Ruth told Emily. They were standing at the fence that separated the two properties. Watery sun filtered through clouds drifting above their heads. Sarah sneezed and delicately held a Kleenex against her nose. Emily slid her hands over the fence's smooth pickets.

"Never?" Emily asked.

"Never," Sarah confirmed.

To have hair that long! Why hadn't Emily's mother realized how pretty Emily would look with her hair hanging straight down her back—why hadn't Emily's mother insisted she keep it long, instead of letting her get it cut in a "shag" that left her ears sticking out? Her mother had allowed Emily to make a terrible mistake, and Emily decided that she'd never get her hair cut again; she'd let it grow and grow.

And her hair was long now, reaching to a point between her

shoulders and elbows, thick and perfectly straight. "You have great hair," her friends told her, all the time. Emily knew she spent too much time brushing it, too much time admiring it in mirrors. But her hair was a goal she'd reached, an accomplishment like making the cheerleading squad or getting the only A+ on last week's Spanish test. It was something she could take with her when she left town to start her new life in college. "Eighty," Emily's mother said.

"Ninety," her father replied.

Emily's mother sighed. "A hundred."

Her father received a pension from the government. He had been a soldier in Viet Nam for a few months when Emily was a baby, and maybe his leaving for the war had been the true start of the trouble between her parents. "He always thought he was such a damn hero," her mother told Emily. "He didn't have to go—he was married, we had you." But for some reason, Emily's father enlisted; he went away and returned with a perforated eardrum. She was young enough then that she didn't remember his absence or his return. He came back to Thedford and did plumbing work and refinished furniture. Emily's mother had Emily's younger brother, Allen. Sometimes at night, Emily heard her parents fighting after they thought the kids were asleep. The fights, as far as Emily could tell, were always about money and her father's drinking. The same thing, over and over, never resolved.

"A hundred and twenty," her father—*Boo*—said. Emily glanced at him. Had he bid up twenty dollars, rather than ten, deliberately or by accident?

"A hundred and thirty," Emily's mother responded.

"One forty," Boo said.

"One hundred and fifty." Emily's mother had two hundred and fifty dollars in her purse—money that could buy Emily and Allen new winter coats, plus enough groceries to let the three of them eat well for a month. Emily had no idea how much cash her father might have wadded in his pocket.

"One sixty." Boo stretched his legs out straight in front of him and crossed his ankles.

"One seventy."

Movement rippled through the audience. People turned toward each other, their shoulders raised in a silent query: How high do you think they'll go?

There were two strange things about Ruth and Sarah. For one, they always wore dresses. Nice dresses, the sort of thing Emily herself wore only to church: cotton fabric patterned with flowers, lace trim on the collars, long sleeves—even in summer—with elastic at the wrists. They wore clean white knee-socks and shiny black shoes. Every day!

"It's because of our church," Ruth said, when Emily asked if they had any play clothes.

The other strange thing was that they were forbidden to watch television. "It's the mechanism of the Devil," Sarah said.

"Television?" Emily asked. They were sitting at the picnic table in Emily's backyard, trying to agree on something to do. "Even Mr. Rogers?"

"Who's Mr. Rogers?" Ruth asked.

"This man who has a show for little kids," Emily explained. "He always puts his tennis shoes on at the beginning, and he has a trolley car who's his friend."

"A trolley car?"

"A little one. Like from a train set. He asks it questions, and it moves, you know, back and forth to answer him, and rings its bell—"

Sarah and Ruth regarded her gravely, as if she'd just proved their point.

Then Emily's younger brother Allen lurched up to the table,

dragging one leg for comic effect. "I'm *bored*," Allen said. He collapsed onto the seat next to Emily. "Mom said you're supposed to entertain me."

Emily sighed. But then she had an idea, inspired by the nightly news her father watched, the exotic names of places like Pnom Penh and Ho Chi Minh Trail that had grown, over the years, as familiar as the names of Nebraska towns. They could play Viet Cong—possibly a babyish sort of game for eleven-year-olds, Emily knew, but since Ruth and Sarah couldn't watch television, and Allen needed to be included, it seemed to be a reasonable compromise.

Standing on the block at the Slave Auction, Emily looked at upraised faces regarding her the way Ruth, Sarah and Allen had years ago when she explained her idea. "Sarah and Allen can be the Viet Cong. That's the jungle, over there. The Viet Cong is always hidden, trying to get the American soldiers. That'll be me and Ruth. Or Ruth can be the Red Cross station, over there." Emily had pointed to the cellar door. It covered a flight of steps that opened into their basement, where her father sat watching television when he wasn't out on one of his plumbing jobs. Ruth quickly fulfilled the duties of the Red Cross, stocking an old tool box with Band-aids and aspirin pilfered from their medicine chest, then joined Emily as a soldier.

The four of them spent the rest of the summer engaged in the game, tracking each other through the yards, hiding behind trees and bushes, trying to hit each other with old walnuts dropped by the tree between their houses. They began digging a shallow trench until Emily's father saw what they were doing and yelled at them. "What the hell are you kids up to?" Emily had known, somehow, she shouldn't explain the game—she shouldn't tell her father that Allen and Sarah were Viet Cong, that their property had transformed itself into a foreign land, oaks becoming palm trees, the overgrown spot to the north of Ruth and Sarah's now named the jungle of Da Nang, Emily's father's own garden a rice paddy they were careful to avoid. "Just messing around," she said to her father. The others stood behind her, silent. Sarah had dirt smeared on her hands and across her cheeks.

"Well, cut it out," her father had said. "Jesus. You're killing the grass."

"One eighty," said Emily's mother.

"Two hundred," her father said, jumping by twenty again. Emily wanted to shut her eyes. Last year, he dropped out at two hundred. He must have brought more money this time, scraped together from the pension and the odd plumbing jobs he took. Lately he'd kept up on the child support payments, so no one could accuse him of using money that actually should belong to Emily's mother.

"Two ten," Emily's mother said. Two ten was too close to two fifty. Goosebumps broke out on Emily's arms and the bare skin of her legs. What if her father bought her? What would he ask her to do? He'd called three or four times since last year's Slave Auction, inviting Emily and Allen to his new house for dinner, but Emily always had something else to do—cheerleading practice, play rehearsal—and Allen refused to go by himself. If her father bought her, it would be the first occasion she'd spent time with him since *the incident*.

"Two twenty," her father said. And then it took only seconds for the numbers to ratchet up to two hundred and fifty. Her mother said them. Emily could see her fingers gripping the purse, turning white. Everyone waited. A bead of sweat crawled from under Emily's arm and slid along her ribs.

"Do I hear two sixty?" Dr. Donaldson asked. He didn't bother with the bullhorn.

"Three hundred," Boo said, extravagantly. Emily shut her eyes. *Jesus*, she thought. *Jesus*.

Dr. Donaldson cleared his throat. "Do I hear three ten?"

The room was silent. Emily's mother looked down at her lap.

People in the rows behind her glanced at each other. Someone coughed. Three hundred dollars was the most money ever paid for a slave. "Well, then," Dr. Donaldson said. "Emily Ambrose, sold to her—sold to Walter Ambrose."

Emily went down the two wooden steps that connected the auction block to the floor. She was supposed to sit next to her father; she knew the rules. She took the seat in the middle of the three empty ones between her parents. Her father reached across the chair between him and Emily. "Boy, sweetheart," he said, smiling. Smiling, as if this whole scene had been something perfectly normal! His fingers touched her elbow. "You cost me an arm and a leg."

But even with their Viet Cong game as a distraction, something about the *mechanism of the Devil* drew Sarah in. Once Emily saw her in front of Larsen's Appliance Mart, transfixed by the TV in the display window until Ruth pulled her away. And even stranger was the afternoon in late summer when Emily went to the basement, looking for Allen. Though the basement was only one big room with a cement floor and cement block walls, her father referred to it as his "den." He sat down there to watch the news on an old TV with rabbit ears on top. It was chilly in the basement, even in summer, so her father wore an old parka. He set his drink on a rusty TV tray positioned next to his chair.

Emily paused at the bottom of the steps. Her father was watching a segment about the war. Gunfire popped in the distance behind the newscaster's voice, and Emily listened to the names that had become places surrounding her own house: Ho Chi Mihn Trail, Saigon, Da Nang. Her father lifted the drink to his mouth and lowered it. More gunfire. And behind her father, a few feet from the cellar door that led to the basement from outdoors, stood Sarah. Emily blinked, surprised. She realized Sarah must have snuck, like the Viet Cong, into the house. Sarah had lifted a few strands of her beautiful hair up to her mouth and was chewing on the ends, distractedly, her eyes focused on the TV. *The mechanism of the Devil.* Emily stood, facing her father and Sarah, watching them watch the television, her father lifting the drink to his mouth, Sarah behind him lifting her hair. She didn't think her father knew that Sarah was there. And, for a moment, neither of them noticed Emily. Their eyes were fixed on the television set.

Then Sarah saw Emily and waved, nervously. Emily waved back and waited until Sarah slipped out the cellar door before going back upstairs. Her father remained, staring at the TV, oblivious to the girls who had come and gone around him.

Ruth and Sarah were gone now. Their father had preached in an old church that ultimately became Thedford's community center. Only a few people from town had attended his sermons. "Crazy Bible thumpers," her father muttered about Ruth and Sarah's parents, even though he was pleasant enough when they ran into each other outside. Last winter, a week or so after *the incident*, Ruth told Emily they were moving. "To Oklahoma," she said. "There's a congregation there that needs a preacher, so we're going."

Emily nodded. They were crossing the street, headed west. Ruth went to the Christian Academy a few blocks away from Thedford High, and she and Emily normally walked to and from school together, maintaining an oddly casual friendship after all these years. Though they never mentioned it, surely Ruth and Sarah were aware of how the fights between Emily's parents had escalated, the skirmishes erupting and sometimes spilling out onto the side yard, an area Allen had christened the DMZ. Even now, sitting here between her mother and father in Thedford High's lunchroom, conscious of the whole hushed audience around them, Emily wondered if Ruth's family heard the last fight: her mother's scream, Emily's own shouting, the car starting up in the middle of the night to go to the hospital. Was the real reason they left to get away from Emily and her family, the house that hummed with the canned laughter of television, a place where you could hear horrible things going on?

The night of *the incident*, her parents began arguing at dinner. It was two days before Christmas. The whole house smelled pleasantly of pine from the tree in the living room, decorated with glass ornaments, popcorn strings, and a brittle, fragile chain of red construction paper that Emily had made in first grade. Snow piled in the corners of the windows. It was a perfect-looking scene, except that Emily's parents had been arguing. Emily pushed cut-up slices of pot roast and carrots around on her plate. They all had glasses of water, except for her father, who drank from a sweating can of beer.

"We've got to economize, Willa," her father said. "We've already spent enough money on Christmas this year, we don't need to go getting presents for the *house*, for Chrissakes." At issue was the new slipcover for the sofa Emily's mother had bought that afternoon, along with matching throw pillows and two crystal figurines she placed on the knickknack shelf Emily's father had built and hung in the living room. "There was nothing wrong with that couch, nothing."

"I *know*," Emily's mother said. "That's why I just bought a cover for it. And those figurines are collectibles, it's better than putting money in the bank, the way they'll go up in value."

Her father shook his head, exasperated. Emily and Allen exchanged glances. "May we be excused?" Emily asked.

"Don't you want desert?"

"No, thank you," Allen said. They put on their coats and hats and escaped outside into the cold. Hazy strips of clouds rushed across the sky. In the house behind them, light glowed in the dining room window. Emily could see Ruth and Sarah, their mother and father, seated around a table, heads bowed and hands clasped. Beside her, Allen sighed. "They're so quiet," he whispered.

"I know," Emily said.

When Emily and Allen came inside, their parents must have declared a cease-fire because they were both sitting in the living room. Emily's father was drinking beer and reading the paper, her mother knitting on the couch. The new slipcover did look nice, Emily thought—a cream-colored plaid design on a navy background. The couch's original upholstery was scratchy and light brown, worn in spots. The two crystal figurines, a bird and a tiny elephant, glowed in the light from the Christmas tree. *Normal*, Emily thought. She wanted everything to stay the way it was right at that moment.

A noise woke Emily: the sound of something falling. She sat up. Her parents' voices became audible, the deep rumble of her father, her mother, shrill. She got out of bed and padded quietly down the stairs.

They were in the kitchen. Beer cans sat on the counter. One of the kitchen chairs lay tipped on its side. Her mother held something clasped in each hand, something her father was trying to wrestle away from her. It reminded Emily of times Allen closed his fist over an item Emily wanted and she'd have to pry his clenched fingers, one by one, from the treasure, both of them sweating with exertion. "Goddamn knicknacks," her father was saying, loudly. "Goddamn doodads."

"Stop it, Walt," her mother said. "*Stop it.*" They didn't notice Emily in the doorway. The overhead light blazed down, casting shadows on their faces that made them look old and ugly. Emily's heels rested on the wood floor of the dining room, her arches and toes against the kitchen's chilly linoleum. The air felt icy cold, as if a window were open. She folded her arms over her chest.

Her father crossed the kitchen floor, yanked the handle of the junk drawer, and pulled out the little hammer he used for fixing things around the house. "They don't mean *anything*," he said.

Emily's throat felt clogged. Was her father going to tear the knickknack shelf off the wall in the living room? Use the claw end of the hammer to rip stuffing out of the couch? He pulled at Emily's mother's hand again. She lifted her arm. They stumbled around the kitchen, breathing heavily. And then Emily saw the hammer raise and come down. It struck against the side of her mother's face, by her left eye. Blood erupted where the hammer had touched. Emily's mother screamed. Her hands came open. The two little figurines she'd been holding bounced on the floor and broke.

"Mother!" Emily cried. Her parents' faces turned toward her. The blood on her mother's skin appeared garish and unreal. Her father's mouth fell open, his jaws so far apart Emily could see all his teeth, even the molars in back. The hammer clattered against the floor. He walked toward Emily, his arms open as if he were going to hug her.

Emily backed up. "What the hell are you doing—"

"It was an accident," her father said. His lips and eyes looked wet, the viscous sort of dampness Emily associated with snails and worms. "I didn't mean to hit her." He turned toward Emily's mother. "Tell her, Willa—it was an *accident*."

The day after the auction, Emily had swimming class and Spanish in the afternoon. After school, she was supposed to drive out to her father's house. He wanted her to have dinner and spend the night. Slicing her arms through the chlorine-saturated water of the pool, Emily added up the hours she'd be forced to spend with Boo—eighteen, she estimated, four p.m. to ten a.m., and divided three hundred by eighteen. Over sixteen dollars an hour! She wondered what Dr. Donaldson would spend the money on. Maybe there would be enough for new chairs in the library?

The P.E. teacher, who was also the swimming coach, paced around the perimeter of the pool. When Emily's ears rose above the level of the water, she heard his feet slapping wetly against tile. The splashes and noise of breathing from the swimmers echoed against the walls. "Keep moving," the P.E. teacher called. "Keep moving." The swimmers were responsible for keeping track of the laps they completed, and at the end of class, they stood shivering, wrapped in towels, and told the teacher the number, which he marked on a clipboard. "Good," he said. "Good, good."

Swimming for forty minutes always exhausted Emily, then there was the rushed shower in a big room with six or seven other naked girls who pretended they were unmoved by their own exposure but carefully positioned themselves to hide perceived excesses of baby fat or moles or too-large breasts. In the locker room, Emily squeezed a towel against her hair. Her clothes stuck to her not-quite-dry skin. Denise pulled on socks and carefully tied the laces of her tennis shoes. "What do you think I should make?" she asked, referring to the dinner she would be preparing for her boyfriend's parents. "Something simple, or something fancy?"

"How about something simple, with a fancy desert?"

Denise nodded. "Like pork chops and baked potatoes, then crepes?"

"Crepes would be good." Emily hung her wet towel inside her locker. "I think my mother's got a recipe if you want, you know, to call me—"

"You're spending the night at Boo—at your father's, right?" Denise asked.

Emily nodded.

"So later tomorrow?"

"I think I'll be home in the morning."

"Okay." Denise's hand reached out and hovered above Emily's arm. "Well, good luck."

The drive to her father's didn't take long enough. His house was visible from the highway, positioned at the top of a small rise, alone in acres of land. She slowed and turned onto the long driveway. Her father was sitting on the porch swing. He stood and waved. Emily raised her own hand behind the window and parked the car.

"Hi, Sweetheart," he said. He sounded different than he usually did. His voice was livelier, strangely affectionate, and his face seemed less ruddy, the lines around his eyes and mouth less noticeable.

"Hi," Emily said. She had managed to avoid him for over a year and now speaking to him felt awkward, as if she were visiting with an old aunt in a nursing home, but her father didn't seem to notice.

"Thought what we'd do," Boo said, ushering her into the house, "is have some coffee and visit for a bit, and then we can go out for a bite to eat. There's a little café just opened off the road to Senecca. Then there are some friends of mine I'd like you to meet. That be okay?"

Emily nodded. She looked around the tidy kitchen, full of evidence of her father's notion of the right way to live: everything put away, bare white walls, none of the disorder of family life— gloves dropped on chairs, somebody's keys always misplaced. Vinyl placemats marked four places on the table. Salt and pepper shakers stood precisely in the middle with a tin box, about the size of a file folder, next to them. A stack of photographs held with a rubber band rested on top of the box.

"Sit down," her father said. "How do you like your coffee? Your mother lets you drink coffee, doesn't she?"

Emily nodded. "Cream and sugar."

He set a mug in front of her. All her life he'd ordered them around: *Bring me a beer. Turn up the TV, will you? Move this, move that. Come help me find my shoes.* She'd expected the offer of coffee would come with instructions for her to make some, but he had a pot already fixed.

"How's school?" He sat across from her.

"It's fine."

"It must be better than fine—you're always gone when I call, you know, bake sales or cheerleading or show choir practice." He reached across the table and squeezed her hand. Emily couldn't help herself—she pulled her hand away. He pretended he didn't notice. "I didn't know you liked to sing."

Emily shrugged. "I just do harmony in the background, you know, it's no big deal."

"Well, let me know when the next recital or whatever you call it is, and I'll come."

Emily could see it: the school lobby quiet in the early evening, a table with cookies and coffee in styrofoam cups, the parents of other singers talking in low voices—*From Alliance? I have cousins there. Do you know—?* Her father would come in late, or too loud, or smelling of whiskey, and her life would be ruined, again. "Okay." She decided that she would tell him the wrong month, the wrong weekend.

"Things are going to be different. You can bet on that." He nodded, looking down at his hands, then cleared his throat proudly. "I quit drinking. Two months ago today."

"That's good," Emily said. He seemed to be waiting for more. "That's really good."

"It hasn't been easy—some days I go to three or four AA meetings, there's a late one in Scottsbluff and driving all the way out there kind of takes my mind off things. But I feel so much better, you know, none of those mornings—" He shook his head. "Anyway, I wanted to tell you how sorry I am about that accident with your mother. I'm sorry you saw that. I didn't mean to hit her—I was going to use the hammer on those glass animals she'd bought, but things just got out of control." He took a breath, then continued. "We're supposed to make amends, I mean, those of us in AA, Friends of Bill, and I want to do that."

Emily couldn't quite follow what he was saying. Who was Bill? And shouldn't he be telling Emily's *mother* he was sorry? She was suspicious of Boo's explanation, his new role of the perfect father—he wanted something from her, she was sure, and after she'd given up whatever it was he'd set his sights on, he'd go back to being the way he'd always been. You couldn't change yourself, just like that. It had taken her years to grow out her hair. *Years.* She nodded and lifted the coffee mug to her lips.

"The meetings are real interesting, lots of different sorts of people, young, old, in between. Once you feel ready, you stand up in front and tell your story, what happened when you bottomed out. That means, when you reached the worst point of your life through drinking. Some of the stories people tell—" He shook his head. "There was a woman who left her baby in the car for five hours while she sat in a bar and drank."

"That's pretty bad," Emily said.

"But the people in AA, they don't judge you because they've been down there themselves. After that woman talked, folks were standing in line to give her a hug. I almost spoke at the next meeting, but I don't think I'm quite ready. I just like to sit in the back and listen, then visit after the meeting's over." He sat smiling at her, waiting again. "Well," he said. "Anyway, I know this is a lot to get used to. More coffee?"

"No, thanks."

Boo slid the tin box across the tablecloth. "I was cleaning up the other day and I found this stuff, I thought you might be interested in taking a look." The lid had an old-fashioned painting of a boy on it and was hinged to the side of the box. "Some pictures, and this box of things I brought back from Viet Nam."

Emily frowned. She wondered if he'd noticed their game, years ago. And what was in the box? She'd heard of soldiers taking horrible souvenirs from the war—fingers chopped off Viet Cong corpses, ears. Their glasses, whatever odd objects they carried in their pockets: things you could hold out and say, "This belonged to someone dead."

Her father undid the rubber band around the stack of photographs and handed her a picture. It showed two young men, rifles against their shoulders, leaning on a Jeep. Around them bloomed an exotic landscape—palm trees, tall shoots of grass. The men were smiling. One was blond, the other dark-haired.

"That's me." Emily's father pointed. "Just a couple years older than you are now."

Emily squinted. The face was too small to see clearly. "Interesting," she said, and handed the picture back to Boo.

"This one," he handed her another, "you wouldn't want to show your mom." Here the same young men posed with two pretty Asian girls between them.

"Probably not," Emily said. The girls had long hair, pale skin. They wore short dresses and appeared, the longer Emily studied the photo, incredibly young. Were they—prostitutes? Why on earth was her father showing her this picture? What was she supposed to say?

She set the picture on the table and rubbed her fingers against the knees of her jeans.

Her father shuffled through the pictures for a minute, then put the rubber band back around the stack. "Well, I'm getting hungry. We can take this along to dinner and look through it there. Okay?"

So this would be her slave labor: feigning interest while her father explained photo after photo, while he pulled God only knew what out of the box. Emily sighed. "Okay."

The Roadhouse Café was halfway between Thedford and Senecca. On the ride, Emily felt a twinge in her abdomen—a stomachache from the coffee, or was she getting her period? She stared out the window, concentrating, but the twinge went away.

Whistling, Emily's father swung the car into the parking lot. He seemed so eager to get inside that he left the tin box sitting on the car seat, and Emily didn't tell him he'd forgotten it. Inside, Emily looked around the café. Booths lined the walls. The worn linoleum was clean and the air smelled of cooking meat. It seemed like the sort of place her mother would like.

"Hello, Walter," a heavyset waitress said. "Figured you'd be in for the meatloaf."

"Evening, Doreen. Like you to meet my daughter, Emily."

Doreen smiled. "She's awful pretty. Are you sure she's your daughter?"

Boo laughed. He directed Emily toward one of the booths. "We'll take two of the meatloafs," he called. "If you don't mind," he added to Emily. "I come here a lot—sometimes a couple of us stop by for coffee after one of the meetings, so I know what the best stuff is."

"That's fine."

Doreen brought over two plates filled with meatloaf and mashed potatoes. She set the plates on the table and then slid her hand quickly along Boo's arm. "Enough gravy, or do you want more?"

"Looks fine, Doreen. Plenty of gravy."

"It's nice to finally meet you," she said to Emily. "Walter's in here all the time, talking about how you're head cheerleader and doing so well in school. I said, 'Walter, she sounds too good to be true.' I thought this daughter was something he made up."

Emily poked her fork into the potatoes. "Actually," she said, "I'm not really his daughter. I'm his slave."

"What's that?" Doreen frowned, glancing at Emily's father.

"Three hundred dollars," Emily said. "That's what I cost. Plus, he has to pay for dinner." She smiled at Doreen. "My mother didn't have enough money to buy me this year, so here I am." She wasn't sure what had taken control of her. Was it the Devil, the one the Pentecostal girls believed would reach his invisible tentacles out from the television set and wrap them around your mind? Emily knew she was being obnoxious, testing her father to see how much she could get away with. "I'm the most expensive slave in the history of Thedford High."

"It's a thing the school does," Boo explained. "You know, sells the students as a fund raiser. They call it the Slave Auction. Back when I was quarterback for the Tigers, we made enough money to get three hundred books for the library."

"Oh," Doreen said. "I see." She stepped away from their booth. "You enjoy your meal, now."

"Thanks, Doreen," her father said, infusing the words with jovial good cheer, too loud.

Emily waited for him to shoot her a look or say, "Mind your manners, Missy," but he gazed down at his plate and dug his fork into the meatloaf.

"I know it's probably hard for you to change your mind about me all of a sudden," her father said. They were back on the highway, headed toward Thedford. Emily stared out the front window. The tin box and pictures sat on the front seat between them. "But I wish you'd talk to me, you know, about what you're thinking."

Emily felt something shift inside her, low down—a cramp? She held her breath, trying to sense any texture of dampness between her legs.

A little gas station sat on the edge of Thedford. "Stop," Emily said. "I need to get something."

Obediently, her father signaled and turned. "I'll be right back," Emily said, to keep Boo from getting out of the car and trailing her inside. The bell on the store's door chimed, and the woman behind the counter—Denise's aunt, Mrs. Krejci—looked up.

"Hi, Emily."

"Hi."

No one else was in the store. Emily found the Tampax and took the box up to the counter. Mrs. Krejci was nice, putting the box in a paper sack you couldn't see through instead of a plastic bag, all the time acting like it was nothing. "Denise waiting for you outside?" she asked.

"No," Emily said. "I'm with my father."

Mrs. Krejci glanced out the window behind her. "Oh, that's right." She stared, coldly, at Boo's car. "I heard about the auction."

"Is there a bathroom I could use?"

"Right back there, honey."

In the small bathroom, Emily locked the door. The air smelled of Clorox and Lysol. Would that be a lethal combination? Emily knew there were certain types of cleansers you weren't supposed to mix together because it could cause an explosion. The mirror over the sink was a square of shiny tin, rather than glass. It gave Emily's face and hair a dingy, rippled look.

Her underwear was spotless, but another cramp tugged at her abdomen. She tore open the box. Someone pounded at the door.

"Just a minute," Emily said.

"You okay in there?" It was her father.

She felt her teeth grind together. "I'm fine," she said.

"Just checking to make sure you weren't trying to make a break for it." He laughed, a forced sound.

"I'm fine." Emily felt lightheaded. Why couldn't he leave her alone for *one* minute? "I said I'd be right back! I'm *fine* and I'll be out in a minute." She was yelling; she was sure Mrs. Krejci could hear. Outside the door, her father was probably stepping back, shaking his head like a man confronted with a problem too difficult to understand.

"Okay, Emily. Okay."

When she came out of the bathroom, her father had his back to the cooler. Behind him, festive beer cans gleamed with the colors of the American flag. Mrs. Krejci cradled an elbow in each palm, watching.

Boo took Emily's arm, a little harder than he needed to but not so hard that Mrs. Krejci would notice.

"Night, Emily," Mrs. Krejci said. "Everything okay?"

Emily nodded. The clock behind Mrs. Krejci read 7:45. She didn't know how she could bear the next twelve hours.

For two days after *the incident*, Emily's mother refused to speak. The stitches closing the wound from the hammer looked like black thread—plain black thread that you'd use for mending clothes. Emily longed to touch the stitches, to see if they *felt* the way they looked, but her mother's smothering silence made Emily afraid to stay in the same room. Christmas presents lay unopened under the tree. Emily and Allen huddled in chairs in the cold basement, watching game shows and Christmas specials. Their father was gone and their mother always seemed to be asleep, so Emily heated up cans of Spaghetti-O's or poured bowls of cereal, and she and Allen ate in front of the television.

At the end of the second day, Christmas, while Emily and Allen were watching "Hogan's Heroes," Emily's mother came downstairs. She sat on the bottom step and looked at them. "You're father's going to move out. We're getting a divorce," she said. Her voice was scratchy, the way it sounded in the mornings sometimes.

Allen began to cry. Emily waited, but her own eyes remained dry. She felt stupefied from all the hours of television, the endless images, bright light, rattling laugh tracks. Emily walked over to her mother and touched, as gently as she could, the line of stitches. They had the texture of normal thread, warmed by her mother's skin.

The next place Boo drove was only two blocks from Emily's house—the community center, the former Pentecostal Church where Ruth and Sarah's father had preached. The big cross that had hung above the front door had been removed, but the glass-fronted case where sermon titles and times were announced was still there, used now for listing daily activities. FEB. 20, white letters read. SENIOR LUNCH, 12 NOON. AA MEETING, 8 P.M.

"I thought you'd like to come to one of the meetings," Boo said. "See what we do, meet some of the people here." He looked at her expectantly, giving her another chance to express enthusiasm or at least interest.

"Fine," Emily said. "Whatever." Now the cramps tapped inside her, rhythmically. She wished she'd bought aspirin at the gas station.

Her father got out and slammed the car door. Emily followed him into the building and down a flight of stairs to a room where rows of folding chairs faced a podium. Ten or fifteen people Emily had never seen before stood around, drinking coffee from styrofoam cups. Cigarette smoke hung in the air.

"Coffee?" Boo asked Emily.

She shook her head.

Her father began greeting people. "Hi, Jerry. How're you doing, Linda? Been awhile, Tom. Yeah, my daughter wanted to come along tonight, see what we're all about." Faces turned toward her, smiling, welcoming.

Emily wondered what would happen if she walked up the stairs, out the door, and headed toward home. Would Boo run after her? Would he demand a refund of the money he'd paid at the slave auction? Was there a rule about recalcitrant slaves? If Emily's stature as the most expensive slave ever—the money Thedford High could use for new library chairs—vanished, Dr. Donaldson would look at her, she supposed, with disappointment and regret. Her father thought the people at AA didn't judge you after you'd told them every terrible thing you'd done, but Emily knew that couldn't be true. People *did* regard you differently when they knew what you were capable of. Boo's friends at AA were just better at hiding what they thought.

"Emily, this is Dwight." Her father introduced a short man with thinning hair. "He's my sponsor."

"Hello, Emily," Dwight said. He reached out to shake her hand. "So you're the daughter I've heard so much about!"

Emily wondered what her father had said. Something like, *I know I drank a lot, but they drove me to it*?

The meeting was called to order. There was a prayer, and then a girl who appeared to be not much older than Emily approached the podium. "Hi, I'm Angela, and I'm an alcoholic."

Everyone around Emily replied in chorus: "Hi, Angela."

Angela told a story about drunken nights in college, leaving parties and bars with men she didn't know, waking up in strange places. The smoke made Emily's eyes water. She'd have to wash her hair tonight to get rid of the smell. After Angela was done, the audience clapped, and then an older man stood up, said his name—Galvin—and told his story. Too much drinking; he hit a pedestrian; his wife left him. Her father stared at Galvin with the same transfixed expression Sarah had worn, staring at television sets, all those years ago. A whole world opened to you, drawing you in.

Galvin finished. Then, to Emily's horror, her father stood and made his way to the podium. The soles of his cowboy boots rasped against the linoleum. The smell of butane flared in the air as someone lit a cigarette. One of the florescent lights overhead buzzed and flickered. Emily's head was beginning to pound. At the front of the room, her father stepped behind the podium. He looked right at Emily. "Hi, I'm Walter, and I'm an alcoholic." She ducked her head and stared at the floor. *Oh, God*, she thought.

"Hi, Walter."

"It's my two-month anniversary of sobriety, and tonight my daughter's here with me to celebrate."

People clapped. Someone called, "Congratulations, Walter!"

I didn't know, Emily wanted to shout. *I didn't know he was bringing me here; the only reason I* am *here is because he paid three hundred dollars.* There was the truth, and then there was some made-up Emily he stood there creating, a fictional, devoted, supportive daughter. Anger propelled Emily to her feet. "Excuse me," she said, edging past the two women sitting next to her. The coffee maker hissed and bubbled. Someone coughed. A bad cramp squeezed at her insides, hard enough to make goosebumps rise on her arms. She approached the podium. Her father took a step back. He lifted his hands a few inches in the air, like a man protesting his good intentions.

"You don't have to say anything, Sweetheart. I don't want to put you on the spot."

He was scared, Emily saw. He was scared to hear what she might say: *He bossed us around. He was always yelling. He hit my mother with a hammer because she bought a new cover for the sofa. She has a scar. He never cared what happened to us; he was always behind on the child support payments, and I'm not here to celebrate anything. The only reason I'm here is because he bought me at the slave auction.*

She stepped behind the podium. The raised faces of the audience regarded her expectantly. She could feel anxiety radiating from her father, tangible as heat coming out of a vent. She breathed in the bad smells of smoke and charred coffee, a combination more suffocating than the food and Clorox scent in the gym during the Slave Auction.

"Honey," her father whispered. "Really, you don't have to talk."

But everyone else was waiting for what she had to say. The power she felt at that moment made her throat ache. "Hi, I'm Emily." She hadn't decided what to say next. The sentence that came out of her mouth, though, made perfect sense. "And I'm Walter Ambrose's daughter." The word they used for their problems was *alcoholic*; the word Emily used for hers was her father's name.

But the Friends of Bill didn't seem to understand. There was a moment of silence. Dwight tilted his head, confused. Emily looked at her father. His eyes shone with relief—it could have been so much worse than this elliptical statement. "I want to go home," she said. "Now."

He owed her. He knew he owed her. "That's fine, Sweetheart. Whatever you say."

Outside, there was the debate about Emily's car, still out at her father's farmhouse.

"I'll just drive you back there so you can pick it up—"

"No," Emily said. People from the meeting started coming down the community center's front steps and milled around them. "Denise can bring me out tomorrow."

"All right," he said. "That's fine." He wasn't going to argue with his friends nearby. He opened his door and picked up his Viet Nam mementos. "I still want you to have this."

She was tired of talking; she just wanted to go home. She took the box. She knew she should say something—*Nice seeing you*, or *thank you for dinner*, or, at least, *goodbye*. Instead, she crossed the street. The unfinished, unended aspect of the evening seemed to keep her connected in some way to her father, as if a string were tied between them, stretching taut as Emily moved away. The feeling of guilt for her own rudeness urged her to turn back. But Emily kept walking. She took the short-cut that led behind the house where Sarah and Ruth had lived. There was still a slight depression in the ground from the trench they'd dug during their Viet Cong game—she could feel it under her feet. Now that Ruth and Sarah were gone, Emily and Allen were the only two people in the world who knew why the land sloped down infinitesimally in that one place. To everyone else, it would be a mystery of nature.

The full moon hung in the sky. A dog barked in the distance. Cold air filled Emily's lungs. She passed the Ho Chi Minh Trail, the Da Nang Jungle, the rice paddy, the familiar terrain of her own backyard. Dead weeds crackled under her feet. Her father receded and receded behind her. She was free—free! She broke into a trot, holding the box against her chest. It was heavier than she'd expected, and as she ran, its metal sides whispered, brushed by whatever unimaginable things it held inside.

Where Everything Begins

So, start here: The moment the boy, James Butler Hickok, first touched a gun and felt the handle fit so righteously well into his palm it could have been grasping *him*, saying, This is who you are. Suddenly, he understood, the way some girls know how to sew by simply touching the needle to cloth, the way other boys could whisper a single word to a wild horse and calm it, just like that.

As a grown man, the pair of Navy Colts defined him, with their handles of ivory that had once been tusks of a beast heavy enough to crush poachers' skulls. The barrels smelled of sulphur and the odor always hung around him, like a warning. Oh, there was talk about bargains he'd made with Lucifer; about the ten men he'd killed—single-handedly—at Nebraska's Rock Creek Pony Express Station; about other things he might or might not have done. No one denies that Custer's own wife couldn't tear her eyes away from him.

Every time he shot a man, he understood anew: This is who you are.

Everything begins. Mark the point where the creek originates, the road starts out, the name descends. A woman said it first: Wild Bill.

Mark his last mistake. But what precisely was his last mistake? The first step on the soil of Deadwood Territory? Indulging that old poker habit? Or sitting with his back to the door of Carl Mann's saloon that fatal August afternoon, sun pouring down outside while locusts in the weeds warned of fall?

How far do you go back?

Jack McCall, insensate to the sun, deaf to locusts, pushed through the saloon doors. By all accounts, he didn't pause. He raised the gun and fired. The bullet went clean through Wild Bill's brain.

Hickok might have heard the killer curse—*Damn you, Wild Bill*—as he fell forward, arms stretched out before him, hands almost clasped in prayer, the way he must have imagined when he'd written earlier that day to his recent but distant bride: "If we never meet again—I will gently breathe the name of my wife—Agnes—and with wishes even for my enemies, I will make the plunge and try to swim to the other shore." Dying, he thought of her and reached out toward that unknown coast.

Ray Sips a Low Quitter

It's Bar Day minus four, early afternoon. Elise stands in the bathroom, vomiting. Afterwards she washes her face, brushes her teeth, and walks, resting one hand against the wall, back into the den where she and Daren have been studying. Under her feet, the carpet feels unusually rough.

"Are you okay?" he asks.

"Yeah," she says. "Maybe I just drank too much coffee." The room is dim and messy—drawn shades, piles of books and outlines on the floor, highlighters scattered like discarded shotgun shells. A pale film of cigarette smoke hovers near the ceiling.

"All right," Elise says, settling into a nest of pillows arranged in one corner. "Now a bilateral contract consists of mutual promises, while a unilateral k consists of a promise on one side and performance on the other, correct?"

"Correct," Daren says. He's still looking at her with concern. "Do you want to take a break? We could go for a walk or something."

"I'm fine." Elise picks up a cup of cold coffee sitting by the pillows and takes a sip. The liquid sloshes dangerously in her stomach for a second, then settles.

"What's *res ipsa loquitur*?" Daren says.

"Latin for *the thing speaks for itself.*"

"Describe the function of *res ipsa* in tort law."

"Don't you sound like a lawyer," Elise says.

"Don't I," Daren says.

"*Res ipsa*," Elise says, "has to do with a presumption of negligence, whether an accident was someone's fault."

"Right," Daren says. "You know Toby and I came up with kind of a joke about *res ipsa*—the whole thing sounds like *Ray sips a Low Quitter*. Like a drink some guy named Ray might have."

"A Low Quitter," Elise says. "That's funny." She knows why he's changed the subject away from fault: he's married, and Elise and Daren are sleeping together. Fault is not something he wants to think about.

Outside, shouts of the neighborhood children rise in the air and the drone of insects, tires on asphalt, fill the hot afternoon. Elise and Daren move together on her bed; she's on top, looking over her shoulder at the mirror he set against the back of the closed door, watching him slide in and out between her spread legs as she raises and lowers herself above him.

She looks down at him, into his huge pupils. "We're very bad," she says.

"Yeah," he says. She feels his hands press against her hips, holding her down as his back arches, his eyes close. "Very bad," he whispers.

Sometimes, staring in the bathroom mirror when she wakes or before she goes to bed at night, she recites a scrap from the litany of law she and Daren have been trying to cram into their brains. *The duty of care a landowner owes to trespassers is—*. Or, *The elements of adverse possession require that the claimant's possession be hostile, exclusive, for the length of time required statutorily—*. Other times she carries on a conversation with her reflection. This reminds Elise of her mother, ironing; Elise would watch her mother waving the bottle of starch and muttering aloud,

"So I said, 'What difference does it make? I mean, really, who cares?'"

"What are you doing?" Elise asked once.

"Thinking out loud," her mother said.

After she'd thrown up, Elise looked at herself in the mirror. *I should be studying harder and not sitting around drinking and screwing a married man.* She watched her lips form the words *screwing* and *married man.* These two facts are ones she tries not to think about, afraid that in the finite space of her brain there's only room for the duties, elements and statutes she has to memorize for the bar. Yesterday, Daren's wife called, looking for him. He'd gone to the liquor store on 27th Street to get a bottle of wine.

"Sally," Elise said, "he's out at the library, running off some old exams, then I think he was going over to Toby's. Do you want me to have him call you if he comes back?" She paused carefully between each sentence, so they wouldn't run together.

"No, I'll just see him when he gets home," Sally said, cheerful, oblivious. Elise didn't think Sally could tell she was drunk.

Later in the afternoon, Daren's friend Toby—a fellow Phi Delt who went to law school at the University of Kansas and is back in Lincoln to take the bar—comes over with the property outline he's been working on. This visit is part of the routine that's evolved in the month before the exam; Elise and Daren study together for most of the day, then Toby stops by and they sit around, complaining, and have a beer.

"Jesus Christ," Toby says. "It's not like the exam tests you over anything that has to do with real life—it's not like you have to give a client an answer the minute he tells you the problem. You say, 'Maybe we've got a case. I'll get my law clerks to look into it.'"

"So that should be the only answer we have to know," Elise says. She finishes her beer and stands, pointing at Daren's and

Toby's bottles. "We just need to know how to say, 'I'll get my law clerks to look into it.' More beer?"

"Not for me," Toby says. "I've got to go over that Civ Pro shit again tonight."

"I'll have another one," Daren says.

Toby is holding the front door open when Elise returns from the kitchen with two Bud Lights. "Don't get drunk, you guys," he says.

"Of course not," Daren says. "We'll go over the Civ Pro section, then we can talk about it tomorrow or Tuesday."

"Okay," Toby says.

Elise and Daren don't study; instead they get drunk. With each beer, the nightmare of the bar exam—which is, after all, only four days away—fades into something smaller and more manageable: a bad dream. . . a dream. . . *it's awhile away; we'll do fine,* they tell each other after the fifth beer. *Who cares if we flunk? We can always take it again in December.*

Elise and Daren became friends a few weeks before graduation. She'd known his name, but she'd never had a conversation with him until Waco Day, a traditional event: the law school seniors rented a bus to take them to a bar called The Sweet Hereafter in Waco, Nebraska, where they did their best to drink the place dry. On the ride home, Elise found herself sitting next to Daren. They were both pretty drunk, like everyone else on the bus, and he started telling her about his wife. She seemed nuts, he said, withdrawn, angry, refusing to talk. He didn't know why. They'd been married six months and things seemed to go wrong from the start.

"She just gets so mad when I don't get the dishes done right after dinner. I tell her I have to study, you know, I'll do them before I go to bed but she still gets mad."

"Hm," Elise said. She was conscious, on the one hand, that

everything he was saying was a cliché—*my wife doesn't understand me* was a line she'd heard in dozens of movies—but on the other hand, she'd never known someone her own age, twenty-seven, who was married and having problems. Up to this point, all her friends were single or if they were married, they acted like everything was perfect.

Law school consisted of sudden, violently intimate friendships—you'd sit by someone in contracts and then you'd be on the phone every night for two hours, talking about Professor Walter's chicken hypothetical or Professor Walter's alleged affairs with students—and inside jokes: impressions of the professors' voices, other students. Sometimes a word: *Tortfeased*, for instance. Or *Palsgraf*, a famous case. So Elise wasn't entirely surprised when, after Waco Day, Daren called her to ask about the tax review session on Saturday, or when they ended up going to Madsen's to shoot pool after the review. They talked about torts, which had been the class they'd both liked best freshman year. "I love *Palsgraf*," Daren said, shooting at and missing the eight ball. "I'm going to get a dog and name him Palsgraf."

Leaning on her cue, Elise tried to remember the case. It had something to do with a train, a porter, and a traveler carrying a sack of fireworks. Boarding the train, the traveler dropped the fireworks (or did he hand the sack to the porter, who dropped it?). The fireworks exploded, causing a chain-reaction of damages, a tipped scale, someone's twisted ankle. Ultimately what remained in her mind about *Palsgraf* was chaos—sparks, fire, flames, and the question of blame: whose fault was this mess?

"Do you want to study for the bar together?" Daren asked.

Elise swallowed. She'd heard horror stories about the bar exam—*Buddy Mitchell was on Law Review and he took the bar twice and failed it, he just choked.... I heard some girl from the class of '99 had a job with Barston Edward lined up, but they dumped her after she failed the bar and now she's selling real estate*—and in her own life, the exam loomed as such an obstacle that it precluded any idea of what would happen afterwards. She had to get a job, of course, act like an adult in high heels and suits, but the exam seemed like a wall she couldn't see beyond until she walked right up to it. She imagined this was how prisoners who've planned an escape from jail must feel. There's the escape—then what?

"Sure," Elise said. She leaned over the table, aimed at the eight ball, and watched it roll into the corner pocket.

"I owe you a beer for that," Daren said.

They split a pitcher and watched the sky outside darken. Daren walked Elise to her car and she was only a little surprised when he said, "You're so nice," and kissed her.

They begin studying together in June. Daren comes over to Elise's apartment with his BarBri books and a six pack. The air conditioner isn't working and they slump against the wall in the living room, deciding who's going to outline what, drawing up a schedule, holding the bottles of beer against their faces and necks.

"I hate tax," Elise says. "I mean, Cezzarini finding the money in the piano was interesting, but the rest of it's just too much math."

"I know," Daren says. "Maybe we can get Toby to outline it."

"Good idea." Elise writes *Toby* on the list of outline assignments and reaches for another beer. All the windows are open but no air stirs through the room; her skin feels damp, as if she's just stepped out of the shower. "Jesus, it's hot."

"I know," Daren says. He's been sitting a few feet away from her but now scoots over like a crab. He sets down his beer and touches her neck with his fingers; they feel cold, removed from his body. Chills bloom on her arms.

"Mm," Elise says. It's the first time he's touched her since they kissed in Madsen's parking lot; she shuts her eyes, thinking vaguely of cost-benefit analysis, the cost of an affair versus whatever benefit it might confer—but ultimately he's the one with something to lose, he's the one who's married, she's just an innocent bystander drinking coffee under a window when a piano falls out on top of her.

By the beginning of July, Daren and Elise are spending almost all their time together, studying, or drinking, or in bed. He leaves her apartment at midnight, goes home to sleep, and returns around ten the next morning. Elise imagines the conversation if his wife complains: Daren, his voice low but firm—*I've got to study*—and the underlying implication: *Do you want me to stay home and fail? Then where'll we be?*

Daren arrives in the morning of Bar Day minus three and Elise—showered, legs shaved—lets him in the apartment and fixes coffee. She feels calm in the mornings, cheerful, hardly ever hungover though she suspects she should be since they've been drinking so much.

"Get this," Daren says, stirring sugar into his coffee.

"Hm?" Elise says.

"This morning, Sally was in the kitchen before she went to work—I guess she didn't hear me when I got up, so I was right behind her before she knew I was there—"

"Yeah?"

"She was looking at a checkbook, at the balance sheet. It wasn't our checkbook—all the entries were in her writing and the balance was over five thousand dollars."

"Five thousand?" Elise says. Sally would've been dressed for her job—she was an accountant—in a blue suit, probably, her blonde hair pinned up. Or maybe Sally had an efficient short haircut. Hearing Daren, she would shut the checkbook, slide it into her purse. "What do you think she's planning to do with it?"

"I don't know," Daren says. "Divorce me, maybe?"

The thought of Daren being single makes Elise a little nervous. Would she actually want to date him? There's an element of silliness to his personality she finds somewhat distasteful. One time, for instance, Elise and Daren had gone to The Mill, a coffee house frequented by beatnik writer types, not law students. While Elise ordered coffee, Daren picked up one of the mugs that lined the walls and said in a wacky, nasal voice, "Coffee, tea or me?" He glanced around, waving the mug. "Coffee, tea or me?" Everyone in the coffee shop stared disdainfully. Elise smiled, gritting her teeth.

This is what she'd have to accept if they were dating: public embarrassment, and sober.

"Don't be crazy," Elise says. "Maybe she's saving up for a car and it's a surprise."

They take their coffee into the study and spend three hours reading torts questions.

Paulsen was eating in a restaurant when he began to choke on a piece of food that had lodged in his throat. Is Dow, a physician sitting at a nearby table, obligated to render aid?

"Nope," Elise says. "No duty." She reads the next question.

Dave is a six-year-old boy who bullies younger children. His parents have encouraged him to be aggressive and tough. Dave, for no reason, knocked down, kicked and severely injured Pete, a four-year-old. What is the most likely result if a claim has been asserted by Pete's parents against Dave's parents?

"Maybe they're liable for negligence?" Daren says.

"Bingo."

By one o'clock, they're famished and feeling virtuous; in the kitchen, making lunch—turkey sandwiches and fruit—Daren says, "I think we're in pretty good shape."

"Yes," Elise says. "Another three hours this afternoon and we'll have torts under control."

"Ray sips a Low Quitter," Daren says.

"What would be in a Low Quitter? Would it be good or one of those gross drinks like an abortion?"

"Oh, it'd be good," Daren says. "Ray's not the kind of guy to drink something gross."

"We should make one."

"All right," Daren says. "I'll make my interpretation of a Low Quitter, and you make yours. Then we'll decide which is best." They begin eating their sandwiches as they walk around the kitchen, gathering liquor and mixers.

"Dibs on the blender." Elise opens a can of peaches, drops four in the blender, adds bourbon, vodka, sugar, ice.

Daren's mixing away on the bar, his back toward her. "Don't look," he says over his shoulder. "This is intellectual property."

Elise laughs. She blasts the blender, pulverizing everything together, and pours it into a tall glass. Not bad, she thinks after the first sip. "Done yet?" she asks Daren.

"Yep," he says. "It's a masterpiece."

"Let me try."

"Shut your eyes," he tells her. "It's part of the test."

Obediently, Elise shuts her eyes. "Here," he says. Elise drinks; it's her own version. "Now taste *this*," Daren says. The second Low Quitter is wonderful—it tastes slightly orange and slightly tart, like strawberries.

"Yum," Elise says. "I could drink that for breakfast." She opens her eyes. "What's in it?"

"Company secret." Daren takes a drink. "I'll make you one."

"Okay." They each have a Low Quitter while they finish their sandwiches, and another one for dessert. Elise begins to feel pleasantly dizzy.

"I'm too drunk to study now," Daren says. "So let's have another one."

"All right." Elise lights a cigarette and leans back against the counter, idly trying to see around Daren's back to determine his Low Quitter ingredients.

"No peeking," he says.

"How could you tell?" Elise asks. "Besides, why won't you tell me?"

He turns, handing her a glass. "Just so I know something you want to."

"Now why would you want that?"

"You're right. We should know the same things, so we both pass or we both fail." He walks over to her, takes the cigarette from between her fingers and taps it out. "Let's drink these in bed."

In bed, Daren lies with his face between Elise's legs, pressing an ice cube from his drink against her and licking away the moisture as it melts. "Ray sips a Low Quitter," he says.

"Don't make me laugh," Elise tells him. She feels sweat breaking out on her face and she shuts her eyes, hears herself breathing hard in the quiet room, moves against his mouth, again, again.

Afterwards, they have another Low Quitter and then Daren calls Sally, tells her he's going over to Toby's for dinner and to do some studying over there. He gives her a phone number that's two digits off in case she needs to reach him. Daren makes another batch of Low Quitters and announces they're out of vodka.

"Let's drink these," Elise says, "and then go to the store." She finds her keys, makes sure the blender's unplugged, and they walk outside.

Staggering down the street, Elise is momentarily awestruck that the sky is still light, that the people in cars gaze through windshields, sober, thoughtful; it seems to her that everyone's stereos should be blaring, they should be shouting, singing along.

"Jesus, I'm drunk," she says to Daren. "What'd you put in those Low Quitters, heroin?"

Daren laughs. They walk a few blocks through air scented with cut grass and gasoline. Elise sees fuzzy figures on porches, overhears dim snatches of conversation.

"Look out," Daren says, pulling her away from a tricycle sitting in the middle of the sidewalk. Elise trips, bumps into Daren, and he staggers a few feet. Swaying slightly, they look at the tricycle, a potential instrumentality of accident, innocent as the scale in *Palsgraf* before it fell.

"Close call," Elise says. They realign themselves and continue walking. The smell of gasoline and exhaust fills her sinuses and Elise is suddenly overcome with dizziness.

"I need to sit down," she says. She collapses onto the sidewalk, her back against the rough brick of the Towne Center Building, and shuts her eyes. They're close to one of the busiest intersections in town; she's aware of little drafts as cars pass.

"Are you okay?" Daren says, but Elise knows he's almost as bad off as she is, there's not much he can do. "Do you want me to get you a Coke or a beer or something?"

"A beer," Elise says and begins to laugh, the idea of beer as a step in the direction of sobriety. She's laughing when a bike cop rolls up. He squeezes and releases the bicycle's brakes a couple times before he speaks.

"What's going on?"

Elise knows she should stop laughing but she can't. "A beer!" she says.

"We're not driving, sir," Daren says.

"You know there are laws against public intoxication," the cop says.

"Of course I know there're *laws*," Elise says, struggling to her feet, scraping her arm on the building. "We're law students, of course we know." She looks down at her elbow. "Ow."

"Elise," Daren says.

"Oh," the bike cop sneers. "Law students."

Cops, Elise thinks: there's an established animosity between cops and attorneys, the professor talked about it in Crim Law—

cops jealous of lawyers' education, power, higher pay; cops fucking up the simplest things like making an arrest and forgetting to recite *Miranda* rights, the suspect freed to drive drunk, steal, murder. Now, of course, this particular cop is in a position to make life difficult for Elise, and she'll think later that it's a miracle, really—because there's a small part of her mind saying *Let him know what you think, he's just a stupid cop*—that she doesn't tell him off.

"I'm sorry, sir, I'm taking some allergy medication, you know? And you're not supposed to operate heavy machinery or anything while you're on it—"

"Elise," Daren says. He holds out his left hand toward the cop. Elise sees his wedding band and realizes what he's doing: he's trying to show the cop they're legitimate, they're married, although why marriage might be a defense to public intoxication isn't clear to her. "My wife," he says. "She's a little worried about the bar exam, you know. She's not herself." He takes her elbow. "Really, there won't be any trouble," he says to the cop. "We're almost home."

They start to walk away, testing the water, since the cop hasn't officially released them—but he hasn't officially detained them, either. They move slowly, carefully, expecting the cop to yell *Stop*, but he doesn't. When Daren glances back and reports that the cop has cycled off, they turn down an alley, sneak back to the liquor store, and pick up another bottle of vodka. Walking home—it's dusk now—Elise feels like a prisoner who's successfully escaped.

"Close call," Daren whispers, trying not to bump against her.

Close call: maybe it's a sign, Elise thinks the next morning. Two days left until the test. She and Daren study hard, spend eight hours quizzing each other, until they're both hoarse from reading questions out loud. Toby stops by, and they talk about civil procedure—depositions, interrogatories, dates for filing. By the time Toby leaves, it's dark. They take a quilt out to the balcony and slide out of their clothes. There's a faint touch of breeze; their arms and legs seem almost invisible. Though the comforter's thick, Elise is aware of cement underneath; it reminds her of their first night, on the living room floor, both of them sweating, carpet scraping at her elbows to reveal new skin, pink and painful when she touched it.

The room where the bar exam is held is in the university union, and, walking in, surveying the lines of tables, coolers of water in back, Elise thinks she may have been in this room before: senior prom, silver crepe paper strung along the walls, romantic darkness, the noise of the band and conversation filling the air.

Now, the room is sterile, too bright. It's ten of eight. Groups of people cluster together, talking in low voices, cracking knuckles, gesturing. It's a little like a class reunion; Elise nods and smiles at people she hasn't seen in the two months since graduation, evaluating who's gotten tan—and, the tan suggesting frivolity, leisure time, may not pass—and who looks prepared. She feels Daren moving behind her, hears him speaking. She wonders if anyone knows about them, or suspects. Do they stand too close together? Does she smile at him too much?

By the second day of the test, Elise has other things to worry about beyond what people might or might not be thinking. She's answered two hundred multiple choice questions; her nose is filled with the smell of lead, and the start of a headache licks behind her eyes. Her palms feel sticky. This final afternoon is devoted to essay questions. She raises her hand to go to the bathroom and a woman proctor walks up to where Elise sits and nods. She follows Elise down the hall and stands in the bathroom, waiting for Elise to come out of the stall. It's like being in jail, Elise thinks. She washes her hands, splashes cold water on her face. Back in the room, Elise reads the last question:

> *Assume that Congress in its quest to balance the budget has passed a special tax on income from the sale of wine, beer, and distilled spirits payable by any entity deriving that kind of income. North Carolina, Iowa and some other states have established state liquor stores as the only establishments where liquor may be purchased. The governors of these states feel that the income derived from liquor store sales should be immune from taxation. As the attorney general, you are asked by the attorneys general of the states affected to join with them as* amicus curiae *in the suit urging that taxation is improper.*
> WHAT WOULD YOUR RESPONSE BE TO THE MERITS OF THEIR CASE? WHAT IS THE BASIS FOR YOUR RESPONSE?

Jesus, Elise thinks, and her heart begins to pound heavily. She has no idea how to answer the question. Be calm, she tells herself, though she really has no clue. State-owned liquor stores? None of the liquor stores she and Daren have gone to this summer were state-owned. But that's not the issue. In the room around her, pencils scratch away; the girl in front of her gently adjusts an earplug; she hears bodies shifting. *What if I don't pass?*

Daren's a couple of rows ahead of her and she looks at the back of his head, thinking of afternoons on damp sheets—only two days ago, she'd heard his voice: *Are you close? Do you like that?*—the two of them driven into bed as a distraction, the affair giving them something else to think about as well as an excuse. *I guess if we don't pass it's because* you know—.

Elise looks down at the question again. WHAT IS YOUR

RESPONSE TO THE MERITS OF THEIR CASE? The thing with Daren was a big mistake, she thinks. Maybe if she'd been alone, she would've gone over the tax section more; maybe she'd be facing this question and thinking, *Oh, an easy one.* She presses the pencil against her lips. She's not scared now—maybe whatever she answers won't really matter. So she places the point of the pencil on the paper and watches her hand begin to move. The first sentence she writes is, "This question is somewhat taxing."

She finishes early, twenty minutes till five. There's no point in sitting, agonizing over her last, silly answer, so she raises her hand; the proctor collects the blue book, nods at Elise, and she stands, picks up her pencils, candy wrappers, pushes the chair against the table, and leaves the room.

She could (should?) wait for Daren right outside the room, but she feels herself forgetting about him; he exists now in the corner of her mind, like a task completed: *Oh yes, I did that.* She wants to be outdoors, away from the artificial air. She walks down marble stairs, through the heavy doors, sunlight warming her face.

She sits on one of the wide stone railings that line the steps and lights a cigarette. Waiting for Daren and Toby to come outside so they can go to Cliff's to celebrate, she looks around the campus, which is quiet; late on a summer afternoon, everyone has found more desirable places to be.

Elise presses the fingers of her right hand into the back of her neck, into a hard knot of cramped muscle. "Ow," she says out loud. Tipping her head to one side, straightening her shoulders, she becomes aware of a monotonous tapping noise, like cracked knuckles, and sees a woman sitting in a parked car across the street. The woman holds one arm out the window and hits the side of the car with her hand. She's blonde, she might be Elise's age or a little younger. Could she be Sally, here to meet Daren—a surprise—after the test?

When Elise raises the cigarette to her lips, she sees her own fingers up close, quivering. The woman tilts the rearview mirror and applies lipstick. She's wearing a t-shirt—surely it's not Sally, she's still at work. Surely.

Retribution, Elise thinks, staring at the car, the last essay question rolling through her mind. Was that last question her punishment? Will she end up failing the exam? Or will her punishment be a phone call from Sally some afternoon, Sally's voice saying *I know what you've done?*

Perhaps the retribution is knowing she's culpable, even though Elise bites gently on her lower lip, willing herself to unlearn the way Daren is in bed, willing the act undone. The woman in the car glances at the Union, then looks toward the Fiji house. Elise shuts her eyes and rubs the back of her neck again, hard enough to make goosebumps rise on her arms. *Res ipsa loquitur*, she says to herself, turning the inside joke back outside, back into what it's supposed to be: a presumption of negligence. Negligence makes her think of *Palsgraf*, though she still can't remember the holding of the case. Was it something about forseeability and causation? Against her eyelids, she watches the fireworks fall, their first burst of flame; she hears the sizzling noise of explosion, gasps from the ticket-takers. The scale is still standing upright. In that significant moment before the accident, before fingers started pointing *It's your fault*, Elise wonders if the porter and the traveler looked up, awestruck, and watched as the train station filled with sulfur and light.

Custer's Last One-Night Stand

Three days past the summer solstice of 1876, a woman came into the Seventh Cavalry's camp, some miles from Greasy Grass Lake. She was blonde, an age between young and old; it was hard to tell in the dark. She'd come for Custer, she said.

His men were drinking whiskey from tin cups. The horses bunched together, asleep on their feet. He asked her to cut off his hair, a liability, he'd found, in this heat. False lighting forked in the sky and he thought of gold veins as he sat on a box, feeling the tug and pull of the comb, the quiet slice when blades came together. Her fingers tilted his head. A breeze lifted the cut hair and cast it over the fields.

He asked if her name was Delilah, and she said no, it was not.

Inside his tent, she lay down. He knelt, his legs making the triangular shape of a tepee. He wrapped her hair around his hand. Gold, like light from lanterns, the flesh of plums, rays of sun; that same sun Sitting Bull had stared into for three days while he bled himself, waiting for the vision to come.

It came: white soldiers fell, like locusts, from the sky. A voice spoke to Sitting Bull. It said, *I give you these because they have no ears. They will not listen, and they are yours to be killed, a gift.*

Custer moved against her, again, again. He thought of the repetitive slicing a pickaxe made against rock, seeking the vein.

Afterwards, she left his tent. The moon hung full overhead, its beams pulling howls from wolves' throats. Their singing lulled Custer to sleep. He dreamed of the following morning: how he'd proceed through the meaningless grass, beneath the irrelevant sky, toward his goal—those hills like curves of a human body, filled with gold like the gold in her hair.

Custer shifted and smiled in his sleep. In the fields, strands of his hair clung to weeds. He did not imagine Indians surrounding his troops, blood filling his eyes and throat, how his shorn hair might save him from scalping because the braves wouldn't recognize *Pehin Hanska*—Long Hair Custer—without his locks. All he saw in his dreams was gold, those hills; he could almost feel the horse's flanks shift between his legs as they moved toward everything that lay ahead, asking to be touched and taken.

Abandon

T hat summer I left Benet and then came back was the summer we let ourselves into abandoned houses. Searching, the four of us—Jemmy, his cousin Carlisle, my best friend Lori and me—rattled down dirt roads in Jemmy's old pickup, early June, corn plants stubbling the fields with green. Now I understand how the abandoned houses led to what happened later—and what preceded the abandoned houses led to them, like stones lined to form a path—but none of this came out till the end of summer. Until then, Lori and I never knew any better.

With Jemmy and Carlisle, Lori and I spent whole mornings looking for a place and making sure the house was really empty. Casing the joint, Lori called it. Boarded windows were a sure sign; peeling paint and no dogs leaping out when we turned into the driveway were good indications but not positive. Jemmy said he liked those ones best, the maybes, those tense few moments on the porch waiting to see if someone answered our knock or hollered back to Carlisle yelling, "Hello! Anybody home?"

The first time we went in an abandoned house was a week after my fourteenth birthday, a month after Lori's. Lori and I had the same name—Lorraine—though she went by the first half of it and I used the second half. Our mothers, who'd grown up in Benet and then went to Ames together for a year of college, planned their whole lives to have daughters who'd be best friends like they were. Anyone in town could tell you the story: it was like the myth of Sisyphus, the same known stone he faced every day, his identical task, the way Lori's mom got married a few weeks before my mom did, then both of them pregnant at the same time. They'd sit on the back porch of Lori's mom's house, drinking iced tea and trying to decide what to name their babies. It was my mom's idea to give us a name that could be split up, and since Lori was born before I was, she got the first half.

On the day we let ourselves into our first abandoned house, I sat in the front of the truck with Jemmy. It was morning, before nine, and a pale haze, not quite fog, hovered over the fields. In front of us, an orange triangle appeared suddenly as an explosion, and Jemmy hit the brakes. "Shit."

The triangle was attached to a horse-drawn buggy: one of the Amish driving into Oskaloosa. Sometimes they moved over so you could pass, but not today.

"Shit," Jemmy said again. His dark eyebrows pulled together like a gathered seam. His hair was dark, too, but his eyes were green—a combination you saw on actors. "I'm gonna honk."

My mother said honking at the Amish was rude; they had just as much right to be on the streets as everyone else. "Look." I pointed to a road, perpendicular to the one we were on, that cut between two fields. "Let's drive down that."

In the back, Carlisle pounded against the window. "What's the holdup?"

Jemmy leaned out. "We're going this way. Rain's idea."

The road was rutted and muddy, no gravel. Jemmy held the steering wheel with both hands. I was conscious exactly how far apart we sat, how the small space between us could be bridged if I put one hand on the vinyl and he set his own on top of it. And what would Jemmy's fingers feel like on the back of my hand? That was something I didn't know, something I wanted to, but Jemmy.... Jemmy was older, twenty; I'd known him almost my whole life because his grandma lived down the street from us and he came over on Saturdays to mow her lawn. The way he'd look at me if he knew what I was thinking was something I didn't want to see.

"So, Rain, you been out here before?"

"No," I said. The road widened slightly and then, ahead of us, I saw a white shape: a garage or barn.

"Must be the back entrance to somebody's house," Jemmy said. "Good job, Rain."

The haze was beginning to lift. Jemmy turned off the truck and we all climbed out. A bird sang in the distance, but otherwise the air was soundless, heavy with silence. My heart thudded in my chest. This yard belonged to somebody, this driveway. "Jemmy," I said. "We should go."

"It's Old Man Bocken's place," Carlisle said. "He's dead, it won't matter if we look around a little."

"How do you know?" Lori asked.

"How do I know what?"

"That he's dead."

"It was in the paper, two weeks ago. Don't you read the paper?"

If Jemmy had said this, it would've sounded like teasing, but Carlisle's tone accused, even when he smiled, like now. He was bigger than Jemmy. The backs of his hands were freckled, and Lori thought his eyes were too close together—but he was Jemmy's cousin, and Jemmy's best friend.

The white shape was a two-car garage, doorless, empty. Behind it stood an old refrigerator and farther on, an unplanted plot of garden. In front of the house, a FOR SALE sign had been shoved into the ground. "See?" Carlisle said.

"Let's go inside," Jemmy said.

Lori and I looked at each other. Up till now, we'd driven around with Jemmy and Carlisle three or four times, after they'd swung into the park one afternoon while we were sitting on a picnic bench, eating popsicles. Lori's was grape and starting to turn her mouth blue, the way she looked in winter when she was cold. Seeing Jemmy, we stopped talking.

"Hi, ladies," he said, leaning out the pickup's window. "Care to go for a ride?"

I saw Lori swallow. Jemmy Richardson—who'd been the star quarterback in high school, who'd even played for the Hawkeyes for a season before he tore the big ligament in his knee and came home to Benet—asking us, me and Lori, to go for a ride. It was like finding a ten-dollar bill on the sidewalk. "Sure," I said, nudging Lori, standing and dusting off the seat of my shorts. Walking to Jemmy's truck, we were conscious of our sudden good fortune, of being chosen. The grass was damp and springy under our feet.

In Old Man Bocken's yard, the lawn was brown already, spotted yellow with dandelions. Carlisle scratched the back of his neck and looked at us. "You girls can wait in the truck," he said, "if you don't want to come."

"Let's go in," I said to Lori.

"All right."

The back door didn't even have a lock. Inside, the house smelled musty. Empty bottles lay on the floor in the mudroom and unwashed dishes filled the sink. Flies swarmed over them and a wasp smacked against the kitchen window, buzzing. "Yuck," Lori whispered. I wondered where Old Man Bocken had been when he died—sitting in the living room, thinking about getting up to wash the dishes? In the dirty bathroom? Maybe he'd been out back, deciding on plants for his garden when whatever it was that killed him cut off his breath and shoved his knees to the ground.

The living room was clean enough, pictures of family and John F. Kennedy arranged on the wall. Lori peered through the front curtains at the yard. I could hear Carlisle and Jemmy talking in the bedroom. "It's a great place," Carlisle said. "The water's still hooked up."

"I don't know," Jemmy said. "For sale, that means people dropping by to look at it."

They walked into the living room. "So what do you girls think?" Jemmy asked. "I want to buy a house, how about this?"

"Well," Lori said. "It's kind of dirty."

"Yeah," I said. A house where someone had died might be haunted.

"But you could clean it up, I guess, if you really liked it," Lori said. "Rain and I could help."

"Sure." I wished I'd thought to say it first.

"What's this room over here?" Carlisle asked.

"Laundry, maybe?" Lori said. They went through a doorway off the living room.

"The bedroom's okay," Jemmy said. "Look." I followed him.

The bedroom had green carpet and panelled walls, a twin bed with a white spread over the mattress. The curtains were blue. When Jemmy opened the closet door, empty hangers jangled like wind chimes and a flesh-colored object, the size of a small fireplace log, fell onto the floor.

"What's that?" Thin leather handles hooked onto either side of it and I moved closer, then stepped back when I realized what it was: a fake leg. "Oh," I said, bumping into Jemmy.

He put his hands on my arms. "It's a prosthesis."

Prosthesis: a word so much more graceful than *fake leg*. His hands rested on my arms, above my elbows. I was conscious of him standing right behind me, so close I smelled his clothes were washed in the same detergent my mom used, I could turn around and see what happened next—.

He pushed aside my hair and I felt his lips against the back of my neck. Something inside me turned liquid and I closed my eyes.

Then he stepped away, picked up the leg like it was a normal thing you'd lift, a baseball bat or tool. "Hey, Carlisle," he called. "Look what I found."

When we were little, Lori and I played together every day, our mothers told us, while they canned peaches or tomatoes or, in the winter, drank coffee and folded laundry, or loaded us into Lori's mom's car for a trip to the grocery store. When I thought back to the first thing I remembered, it was Lori in a pale yellow sleeper, strapped in a car seat next to me, her round face and blue eyes. Lori was like a sister, and I was glad I didn't have a real sister because then I would have to make a choice and decide who I liked best.

Growing up, I found the story of our split name unremarkable, though interesting because Lori and I were the main characters. As I got older, the situation began to seem miraculous—that both our mothers had met husbands at the same time, getting pregnant within a month of each other. What if one of us had been a boy? "What then?" I asked my mom. It was the day Jemmy had pressed his lips against the back of my neck, and she and I were cleaning the kitchen after supper. "What if one of us turned out to be a boy?"

"I guess we just would have tried again," Mom said. She'd been staring out the window above the sink but turned to me and smiled.

"Really?" I tried to imagine myself without Lori, or Lori without me. Alone, I wouldn't have gone to the park, wouldn't have gotten into the back of Jemmy's pickup that first day. I wouldn't yet know Old Man Bocken was dead, wouldn't have felt the brush of Jemmy's fingers as he moved my hair aside.

"But everything worked out the first time," Mom said.

And how could you arrange that? I wondered. Dusk filled the sky outside the window and a breeze pushed into the curtains. A bird sang off in the elm tree and I heard a sound that could either be thunder rumbling or a car turning onto the road that led past our house. Was Jemmy with Carlisle, or sitting in his bedroom, or walking into one of the bars downtown? When would we see each other again?

Lori and I bought malts at the Dairy Freeze and rode our bikes to the park, steering with one hand and holding the sweating plastic cups with the other. Even now, past supper time, heat radiated from the asphalt and the air itself smelled singed. A narrow line of dirt striped the back of Lori's calf. Only a week or two earlier, people had been sitting out on their porch swings, but it was too hot for that now. Instead, everyone stayed inside behind closed doors and windows and ran their air conditioners.

In the park, we leaned our bikes against our usual picnic bench and sat on the table part, resting our feet on the seat. Sitting like that made me think of the Amish in their buggies, straight-backed, feet planted firmly on the buggy's floor, the slow view of fields and the horse's broad flanks.

"Do you think Jemmy is going to buy that house?" Lori asked.

"I don't know. I thought it was kind of gross, with the leg in the closet and everything."

"I know." Lori shut her eyes and twitched her shoulders back and forth. "Maybe Old Man Bocken was looking for his leg when he died."

"Maybe," I said.

I must have been expecting Jemmy because I wasn't surprised when I heard his truck in the parking lot. "Jemmy's here," Lori said.

"Hey!" Jemmy called. His face looked tanner than the last time I'd seen him, only three days ago. "Isn't it kind of late for you girls to be out?"

"It's not late." I looked right into his eyes.

"Want to go for a ride?" he asked. "Carlisle's at home, he's got the flu or something."

I felt Lori wanting to look at me, to exchange a glance that said *Good*. "Sure." I stood up and brushed off the seat of my shorts, like I had the first time Jemmy'd come to the park, the familiarity of the gesture—like putting your hand on your heart to say the Pledge of Allegiance—making it seem like we'd been doing this for a long time.

We all sat in the cab, me in the middle, trying not to lean into Jemmy when he turned. He drummed his fingers against the steering wheel, then lifted a can of Mountain Dew to his lips. "Hey, Lori," he said. "Hand me that bottle in the glove compartment."

Lori pressed the lock. Inside was a mess of crumpled maps, pens, a spilled box of cigarettes, and a flat rectangular bottle of pale liquid. Its label said Everclear. Lori passed the bottle to me and I twisted the lid. The smell of alcohol wafted into my face and my eyes watered.

"What *is* that?" Lori said.

"It's a little pick-me-up." Jemmy poured some Everclear into the pop can. "Have a sip."

"No, thanks," Lori said.

"All right," I said.

The truck slowed as Jemmy looked at me. "Just a little sip," he said.

My fingers brushed his when he handed me the bottle. I lifted it to my lips and drank. It was like swallowing a live coal. Heat slid from my throat to my stomach. My nose began to run. "Oh," I said and sniffed.

We bumped across the bridge over South Skunk River. The sky grew a shade darker as we drove. Jemmy said, "Have another little sip, Rain, and I'll show you something." He handed me the bottle.

"Sure you don't want some?" I asked Lori.

"Oh, I guess," she said. Her eyes widened when she swallowed. Jemmy pointed out the windshield. "See the fireflies?"

Hundreds of them hovered over the fields, their lighted tails blinking on and off. Lori and I nodded. "Now squint your eyes a little, and I'll drive faster. They look like sparklers if you do that."

Lori and I squinted and stared out the window. Jemmy accelerated. Gravel pounded against the truck's underside and the fireflies' blinks, altered by speed, stretched into strings of light.

Jemmy was right: the trails gleaming above the rows of corn did look like sparklers. "Wow," I said. My hand reached out and patted his knee. Jemmy put his hand on top of mine, pressing my fingers against his leg. The road dipped and righted itself in front of us.

When I first heard the name of the drug, *crystal meth*, I thought it sounded pretty—clear, icy, like the glass of chandeliers. In Mrs. Gardiner's fourth grade science class, we had made our own crystals by boiling sugar and water together. Each of us had brought a jar from home, and Mrs. Gardiner circled the room, pouring sugar water into baby food jars, Mason jars, my own black olive jar. Lori held out a squatty container that once held artichoke hearts. Then we each dropped a piece of string in the jar, like a line for fish, sealed the lid, and waited. A week later, sugar crystals blossomed along the string.

"That's how you make rock candy," my mom told me.

Crystal: the shared part of *crystal meth* and *sugar crystals*. But what Jemmy and Carlisle put together was nothing you'd want to eat. They ground down cold tablets, added freon, Drano. Chemicals, flammable and hot, mixed together and cooked in Carlisle's garage while his parents were at work. Jemmy thought an abandoned house would be a safer place to use as a factory.

But I knew none of this, hadn't even heard of crystal meth, the afternoon Mom and I leaned over the dining room table, arranging pattern pieces on a folded length of material. She was making me a skirt to wear for the first day of high school. In the fall, Lori and I would ride the bus to the big new school in South English, a half-hour away from Benet. The fabric, a dark green printed with fossilized-looking leaves, smelled new, like the inside of the store.

I'd picked it out earlier that day at the So-Fro in Oskaloosa, then we'd stopped for lunch at the Halfway Diner, where Mom and Dad went on their first date. Normally I'd be content, moving the tissuey pieces around, knowing I'd have something nice to wear when school started, but this afternoon I felt like a cat stroked the wrong way, all its fur pressed against the grain, disordered. Every time I looked at the clock, its hands were in the same place. I wanted to go to the park and wait for Jemmy to appear.

"Did you know Old Man Bocken died?" I said.

Mom nodded. Pinning the pattern to the fabric, she said, "You should call him Mr. Bocken. It's more respectful."

"All right," I said.

"Don't you remember him when you were little?"

"No."

"He used to ride his horse down the street. You and Lori would run out to the porch and he'd throw candy to you. It was like a one-horse parade."

I imagined a man mounted on a black and white horse, Lori and me staring through the slats of the porch like prisoners peering through bars. Disks of candy spun through air, and the horse's hooves clattered against cement. "He sounds nice."

"He liked to do things his own way." Mom began cutting the material. I looked out the front window. Two women, Amish—I could tell because they wore dresses and little nets over the back of their hair—walked past the house.

"What do you call a group of people, like the Amish?" I asked.

"What do you mean?" Mom stopped cutting and looked at me.

"You know how a group of horses is a herd? Like that."

"Oh," Mom said. "Sects."

"*Sex?*"

"S-E-C-T-S," she spelled. A word like the back half of *insects*. Whenever I saw the Amish after that, I thought of the gold and black bodies of wasps.

After Old Man Bocken's house, after Jemmy'd kissed the back of my neck, Lori and Carlisle always rode together in the pickup's bed when the four of us were together. Lori sat on top of the wheel, staring off into fields, pulling away strands of hair that stuck in the corner of her mouth. Watching Carlisle pick at his teeth, or nudge Lori with the toe of his cowboy boot to get her attention, I wondered if one of us would always be giving up something for the other one, like now, Lori stuck with Carlisle so I could sit with Jemmy. Did one of our mothers do that, to fulfill their plan of two daughters? And which mother, mine or Lori's?

In July, we found a house a few miles outside of Kincross, right on the highway, that looked deserted—a TV antenna swung off the roof and pieces of siding scattered around its foundation. The open garage door showed an empty interior. Jemmy pulled his truck behind the house and we jumped out.

"Anybody home?" Carlisle yelled. The lawn brushed my calves and air around the house had that same depth of silence I'd noticed at Old Man Bocken's. At the back door, Carlisle rang the bell. We cupped our hands against windows and peered in. I saw a kitchen table with a pair of chairs, an empty hallway and living room. Carlisle rang again.

"Door's locked," Jemmy said, twisting the knob.

Carlisle glanced around like a cartoon criminal. He pulled a short flat piece of metal out of his back pocket and poked it into the lock. The door swung open.

"After you." Carlisle motioned us in.

The house was cleaner than Old Man Bocken's; here, somebody had packed up and moved away, though the air had that same hot, closed-in smell. Darker squares on the wallpaper showed where pictures had once hung. Mice scratched behind walls.

"Toilet works," Carlisle said, coming out of the bathroom, tugging at his zipper.

Next to me, Lori sighed.

"Hey, I'm hungry," Carlisle said. "Jemmy, give me your keys and I'll go get us some lunch."

"All right." Jemmy handed Carlisle the keys and some folded bills from his front pocket.

"A hundred dollar bill!" Lori said. "Jemmy, you're rich."

"Whoa," Jemmy said, taking the money back from Carlisle and reaching into his back pocket. "Wrong account."

"Come on," Carlisle said to Lori. "I can't carry everything myself."

From the kitchen window, I watched Lori follow Carlisle to the truck. She climbed inside and sat close to the door.

"We should open a window," I said. "It's hot in here." The waistband of my shorts stuck damply to my skin and sweat crawled down the back of my neck. When I pushed the window above the sink, it wouldn't budge.

"Here," Jemmy said. He pounded his fist once against the frame, then slid the window open. Outside air flowed through the screen.

"I like this place better than Old Man Bocken's," Jemmy said. "What do you think?"

"It's a lot nicer. But there's no *for sale* sign. Maybe it's not for sale."

"Places like this are always for sale." Jemmy turned the kitchen faucet. Rusty water dribbled out, then the pipes rattled and a clear stream of water splashed into the sink. He rinsed his hands. "It's cold." He touched my cheek with his wet fingers, slid his hand through the water, then stroked my throat, his eyes on mine. Water sparkled on his skin. He drew his index finger across my lips, wet his hand again, and slid it beneath the hem of my t-shirt, against my stomach. In my chest and moving down, a trail of heat rippled like swallowed Everclear.

"Oh," I said.

"Rain," Jemmy said. His lips brushed my cheek, his fingers traced circles around my nipples. Floorboards creaked as I shifted from one foot to another. "Some afternoon I'll come get you and we can go for a drive, just the two of us."

❀

On the outskirts of Benet, a brick ranch house stood in a plot of perfectly green grass. The driveway that led to its front door was crushed rock that sparkled in the sun. Inside, the kitchen was probably spotless: white cupboards, white countertops. Jemmy and I could stand on the clean tile floor, our arms around each other. "For Sale by Owner" said a sign nailed to the big oak tree out front.

"How about that one?" I pointed. "It looks really nice."

Jemmy barely glanced at it. "Nah. Too close to town."

By the end of that summer, Jemmy and Carlisle had become something Lori and I never talked about. When Lori thought of them, she remembered the smell of Carlisle's sweat, how sitting in the bed of the truck hurt the back of her legs, wind and dust in her eyes. She was always waiting for me to turn away from Jemmy and look at her, waiting for our friendship—which had been stretched like a rubber band—to snap back to its normal shape, waiting for the drives and the summer to be over. Carlisle and Jemmy were like a disagreement we'd had and didn't want to bring up again.

A few weeks before that, early August, we were sitting on Lori's front porch, looking through the Sears catalogue for school clothes.

"Do you remember Old Man Bocken from when we were little?" I asked.

"He rode his horse past your house and he'd throw candy to us," Lori said. "The horse's name was Buster."

"Buster," I said.

"The candies were always broken up because they'd land on the sidewalk."

"What kind of candy?"

"Butterscotch and cinnamon disks. You took the cinnamon disks and I took the butterscotch." Lori pointed at a blonde model wearing a denim shirt and khaki pants. "Do you like that?"

"Mmhm," I said. "That would look good on you." A fly buzzed around my face and I knocked it away. The lawn in front of Lori's house was turning brown from heat, sharp and stiff, unlike the springy grass we'd walked across in the park the day we'd first gone riding with Jemmy.

"He used to do that for our mothers, too," Lori said.

"Who?"

"Old Man Bocken," Lori said. "He used to ride his horse by your mother's house and throw candy. It was a different horse then. Buster's father, I think."

"Really." I shaded my eyes and looked down the street.

"And different candy," Lori said. "Peppermint and horehound."

"*Whorehound*?" I flipped through a few pages of the catalogue.

"That would go with your skirt." Lori tapped a picture of a short-sleeved green sweater.

"Yeah."

A blue Dodge pickup, shiny, new, fishtailed as it turned onto the street and squealed to a stop in front of the house. Jemmy and Carlisle stepped out.

"You got a new truck!" Lori said.

"Thought it was about time." Carlisle slammed the passenger door. His face was red and sweaty. "Look at those tires." He kicked the right front one so hard the truck shook a little.

"Take it easy," Jemmy said. He smiled at me. "We're going to break in the engine. Want to come?"

Carlisle squinted at Jemmy.

"Sure." I started for the truck, expecting Lori to follow.

"Rain." She was still sitting on her porch. She looked at me, then at Carlisle, like she was trying to tell me something. "I want to let Mom know we're leaving."

"No time for that," Carlisle said. He opened the door. "Hop in if you're coming."

I climbed in the cab. Lori stood up. The catalogue lay where we'd left it. I motioned for her—*Come on*—but the sun must have been reflecting off the windshield so she didn't see me, didn't wave or shake her head or look like she might change her mind. The screen door slapped behind her when she went inside the house.

"We'll be right back," I said to Jemmy, "won't we?"

"Sure."

The new truck was air-conditioned, but even with the vent pointed straight in his face, Carlisle still sweated, giving off a scent of rubbing alcohol and something faintly metallic. I sat between them and kept my face turned to Jemmy. He tapped his fingers on the steering wheel. "So, where do you want to go?"

"Mexico," Carlisle said. He reached under the seat and pulled out a bottle of Everclear.

"Sure," Jemmy said. "That okay with you, Rain?"

I knew he was kidding. "Fine with me."

Jemmy turned on the radio. The Eagles sang "Hotel California." Carlisle drank Everclear and smacked his lips. His leg pressed against mine and I moved closer to Jemmy.

A few miles past Oskaloosa, Carlisle fell asleep, head against the windshield, mouth open, the Everclear bottle wedged between his knees. In the fields around us, corn stood high enough to hide in; wasps hovered around fence posts. Toward this time of year, wasps' taste turned from the sweetness they crave in spring to meat, chopped-up hotdogs now replacing applesauce in the wasp traps swinging from the rafters of our back porch.

"Hand me the bottle," Jemmy said, "so it doesn't spill."

Carlisle didn't move when I pulled the bottle away from him. Jemmy took a drink and held it toward me. "Pick-me-up?"

"Sure," I said.

We must have been close to the Missouri border when yellow butterflies erupted from the ditch like handfuls of tossed confetti. They filled the air around the truck in a dense cloud as if we were driving through a snow storm.

"Look at that!" Jemmy said.

The butterflies rose, rode currents of wind, sailed beyond sight.

I wished Lori were here to see it—Lori in the bed of the truck with Carlisle, her palms up like she was checking for rain, looking at the butterflies, smiling. But Lori was in Benet, left behind, as we left the flock of butterflies behind, growing smaller and then disappearing in the rearview mirror.

"We're not really going to Mexico, are we?" I asked. Jemmy and I had been passing the bottle back and forth. I let my leg press against his; I let my hair brush his arm. We'd been on Highway 63 for a while and I guessed we should probably turn around soon so I'd be home before my parents got too worried.

"There's something I want to show you," Jemmy said. "But it's a ways away. Actually it's in Missouri."

"Missouri!"

"They have these underground caverns, it's nothing like you'd see around here."

"Jemmy," I said. "I have to go home."

"How about we call your parents when we get to Jefferson City and tell them where we are, then we'll drive back to Benet tomorrow? Just tell them we're taking a little vacation." He slid his hand under my hair and stroked the back of my neck. When he touched me like that, I felt like closing my eyes.

"Jemmy, they'll kill me."

He smiled. "If they say they're going to kill you, we'll just keep going."

Jemmy flicked the turn signal, took an exit, and pulled into a parking lot, stopping next to a phone booth. It was dark enough that I had to squint to see the motel: it was low, painted dark brown. The only light shone in the office window.

"It's too late to see the caverns tonight," Jemmy said, "so I'll get us a room and we can go first thing in the morning."

Carlisle and I stared out the front window and waited. Across the highway was a Greyhound bus station and two buildings with

Budweiser lights in the windows. Carlisle switched off the air conditioner and rolled down his window. Humid air filled the cab.

Jemmy returned and led us to room 45. He opened the door, sent Carlisle off for ice and pop, and went back outside. I sat on the bed, staring at the phone. I had to call my parents, but the thought was like Carlisle's leg pressing against mine, something I wanted to ignore. Maybe Lori had told them I was with Jemmy and Carlisle. Then they wouldn't worry.

But the truth was, I knew I was already in so much trouble there was no point calling and hearing it confirmed. If I called, they'd tell me to come back right this minute and I didn't know if I'd be able to make Jemmy do that.

Outside, Jemmy and Carlisle stood by the truck. Wasps hovered around shredded butterfly wings that waved from its grille. The sun sank into the horizon, and from the fields around the motel rose the sad sound of crickets.

"I'm fine," Carlisle said. "Give me the keys."

"No." Jemmy put one hand against Carlisle's chest, like he was going to push him, then he saw me. His arm fell along his side. "So, Rain, did you call your parents?"

"No," I said. "Since we're going to be home tomorrow, anyway."

"That's right," Jemmy said.

Carlisle kicked rocks with the toe of his cowboy boot, hands fisted in his back pockets. "I'll be over there," he said, nodding across the highway toward the bus station and the bars, "if you change your mind."

"Carlisle's mad, isn't he?" I asked Jemmy as we walked back in the room.

"He just gets like that sometimes. He didn't want you to come along."

"Mm." I sat down on the bed.

"Want a drink?"

"All right."

Jemmy scraped plastic cups through the ice bucket, then poured in Everclear and Seven-Up. He handed me a glass and stretched out on the other side of the bed. I was glad Carlisle was gone. The drink made me sleepy and I shut my eyes.

"Rain," he said, nudging my leg with his foot.

"Yeah?"

"What would you say if I told you I'd done something real bad?"

I thought he meant fighting with Carlisle, wanting to shove his own best friend and cousin. It didn't seem like that bad of a thing to me. "You probably had a good reason," I said.

He laughed. "I guess." He lay on his side, looking at me. Then he took the drink from my hand and set it on the nightstand. He slid my shorts down my legs and unzipped his jeans. I didn't know where to look, what to do with my hands. The bedspread felt stiff, like it had been dried on a clothesline. Jemmy stood, pulled off his jeans, and then got back on the bed, positioning himself between my legs. We kissed until I was twisting underneath him, and then he shifted, pushing inside me.

The pain was like a slap in the mouth that makes orange explode behind your eyes. "Oh," I said. Jemmy's weight pressed and moved away, then pressed again. Each time he pushed, I pulled back, but there was no place to go, I was pinned between him and the mattress. I took a deep breath, then another. My fingers rested in the small of Jemmy's back, on his hot skin, the precise bones of his spine.

"Rain," he said. He made a noise in his throat, arched his back. I touched the smooth muscles of his arms. Above me, his face, eyes closed, then I felt that part of him inside me pulse twice, three times, like a firefly blinking. He rested all his weight on me. His lashes brushed my skin. Breathing his scent of skin and shampoo, I thought, no one knows him as well as I do right now.

Jemmy rolled away and lay on his back. His eyelids fluttered, like he was trying to stay awake. He touched my arm. "You okay?"

"Sure," I said. It was cold in the room and I felt alternately exhausted and jittery, the way I'd felt that afternoon Mom and I were cutting out my first-day-of-school skirt. I drank the rest of the Everclear and Seven-Up left on the nightstand. Beside me, Jemmy made a noise and turned onto his side. I wanted to talk to Lori.

I pulled on my clothes. Jemmy'd left a pile of quarters by his wallet on the dresser and I took five.

In the phone booth, bugs smacked against the light. I pressed quarters into the slot and dialed Lori's number. The phone rang three times before it occurred to me that I must be drunk—it was way too late to be calling, I should have thought of that. But then Lori picked up. "Hello?"

"Lori," I said.

"Rain! *Rain.* Where are you?"

"At a motel. In Missouri. With Jemmy and Carlisle. Are you mad?"

"No, of course not. Are you all right?"

"Yeah. I have something to tell you—"

"Wait. My mom's here, she wants to talk to you."

"Your mom?" Silence, then Lori's mom's voice. "Lorraine," she said, giving me both our names. "Are you all right?"

"Yes, of course, I know I'm probably in a lot of trouble—"

"You need to come home right away," she said. "Some people need to talk to you about Mrs. Gardiner."

"Mrs. Gardiner? You mean the teacher, Mrs. Gardiner?"

"Yes. Do you know anything about that?"

"About what?" I wanted to talk to Lori about Jemmy; I didn't want to talk to her mother about one of the teachers at the grade school.

"Where are you?"

"In Missouri."

"Where in Missouri? Do you know?"

"Yes, I know." My voice came out louder than I intended. "Yes. In Jefferson City."

"And you're with the boys?"

"Yes," I said. "We're coming back tomorrow." It sounded like Lori's mom covered the mouthpiece with her hand. "Can I talk to Lori?"

Her mother said, "No. You've got to get away from them, right now. They're very dangerous."

I laughed.

"Rain, do you have any money?"

"No."

"Is there a bus station around?"

"Yes," I said. "Across the street."

"Go over there. Don't let the boys see you. I'll call the bus station and charge a ticket for you to Cedar Rapids."

"We're coming back tomorrow anyway," I said. There were some taps, the phone changing hands.

"Rain," Lori said. Her voice sounded stretched out, like she was crying. "Rain, they think Jemmy and Carlisle killed Mrs. Gardiner and stole her truck. You've got to get away from them."

Something in my throat swelled up so that it was hard to swallow. "Killed Mrs. Gardiner?"

The operator came on the line and said our time was up.

I waited in the bus station until dawn. Twice I went to the bathroom and sat on the toilet, dabbing gingerly between my legs. Blood spotted the tissue. In the waiting room chair, I slouched down so my weight rested at the bottom of my spine.

No one took the seat next to me on the bus. Beyond the window, I watched the sun rise to illuminate a hilly landscape that gradually flattened. I wondered if Jemmy were awake now, if he'd opened his eyes and said my name, if he and Carlisle were on the road already, on their way back to Benet or headed to Mexico. Jemmy killing somebody! It was hard for me to wrap my mind around that idea when I kept seeing him leaning out of his pickup truck—the old one—and smiling, or his face above me last night, the way his voice caught when he'd said my name. *Rain*. Jemmy when he was my age now and me as a little girl, standing on my own front porch, watching him drag the lawnmower out of his grandmother's garage. I would've been seven or eight and I stood there waiting until he waved to me, his brown arm an arc against the blue sky.

That's how I thought of him, even after the trial when the sheriff led Jemmy and Carlisle from the courtroom, both of them in jumpsuits the color of traffic cones, wrists handcuffed and legs chained, Carlisle's head shaved. By then everyone in town knew about the crystal meth they'd been selling, the search for a place to set up their own lab, me and Lori like decoys along with them. We made the drives around the country look innocent, purposeless, just the football hero being nice to a couple of little girls.

I wondered if Jemmy had waved to Mrs. Gardiner, too, when she'd come to the door to answer their knock. "Jemmy!" she would've said, holding the storm door open. She didn't know they'd been up all night, testing their latest batch of crystal meth. Jemmy and Carlisle pushed her into the house, through the living room and into the kitchen, where one of them shot her. They blamed each other. It was morning; they took her truck and drove around for hours and hours, deciding what to do.

Around town, people said that I'd been kidnapped and held hostage, that it was a miracle I'd gotten away. I'd struggled a gun out of Carlisle's hands, or untied my bound wrists and picked the lock of a car's trunk from the inside to escape. I'd run four miles barefoot and hitchhiked home. No one believed that I'd just walked away from them.

And no one knew how I'd stood in the phone booth in Jefferson City after the connection was broken, holding the receiver against my chest. Crickets droned in the fields; cars roared past on the highway. I considered the note of desperation in Lori's voice. *Get away from them.* I stared at the door of the room where Jemmy slept. It took me a while to decide what to do.

Transubstantiation

L ate October, past dark, the fall when Mars hangs closer to earth than it has been in sixty thousand years. Sixty thousand years! my father repeats nightly, eternally awed. In its proximity to earth, the Red Planet doesn't look red at all; it winks like a large golden star in the sky.

Besides the apparition of Mars, this fall is significant because my father—an undemonstrative man, not much of a talker—is continually trying to *give* me something: A beer stein from my tenth high school class reunion he found while cleaning the basement. Boxes of Kleenex he picked up on sale at Walgreens. Had I seen this article in the paper he clipped for me? Did I need some vegetables from his garden? Surely I could use some vegetables.

He's worried my marriage is failing. He doesn't say he's worried. Instead, he hands over boxes of Kleenex; I see a certain look on his face when I turn and catch him watching me. A stillness, the expression of a man listening to a sound in the distance and trying to determine its origin. Thunder? A train? The last locusts of the season?

He doesn't ask, though certainly he's curious as to why I've been coming back home every night after dinner. I take a walk on Sheridan Boulevard, the long flat street two blocks north of my parents' house. The walk, a full four miles from one end of Sheridan to the other and back, consumes an hour, sometimes more, depending on how long I linger in front of houses where friends of mine used to live, boys I dated, boys I slept with. Dusk comes on moments earlier every night, the air growing incrementally cooler as the season winds down.

Still, it's warm for October, warm enough for us to stand in the garden coatless. Over the years, my father's garden has swelled to consume the entire east side of the yard. Beans climb poles that once supported clothesline; raspberry bushes tangle in the fence that separates our property from the neighbor's; cornstalks crowd against the garage. The garden sprawls over the area where our pets were buried, so among the monstrously large chive plants and the peony bushes—transplanted from the farm where my father grew up—lie the various grave markers: two bricks for Emerson, a paving stone for Lucy, rocks from a creek bed for Yogi and Beth.

The animals have all been dead for years. They were my childhood pets.

My father rustles through rows to the garden's back corner. His flashlight zigzags across the ground like a dog scenting. I stand by the graves, breathing in the smells of fall: dirt, leaves, wood smoke.

How's Josh? my father asks.

Fine, I say.

Do you want to take some vegetables for him?

He's out of town, I say.

Oh.

My father stoops. Vines rustle, stems snap. He gathers; I wait. My feet sink into the soft ground. The light of Mars washes over the bricks, the stones, the rocks.

The flashlight swoops, suddenly, across my shins and stops by Lucy's paving stone. Next to the stone, an old Folgers can holds a bunch of zinnias. My father says, She died on the twentieth of October, right?

Yes, I say.

That's what I thought, he says.

He likes to commemorate the anniversaries of the animals' deaths. He had to leave behind the grave of his own favorite dog, Fanny, when the farm was sold after my grandparents died, and I think his attention to the graves in his garden is a form of contrition. He wouldn't like the word *contrition*, I know, with its religious connotations; he's agnostic, a man who reacts to stories of faith with a wave of his hand, as if he's shooing away flies.

The flashlight swoops back to the spot where he's standing, by the tomato plants. He says, So Josh's out of town?

I hear the flashlight rattle against one of the tomato cages, and then the quiet thud of a tomato hitting the ground.

I was just thinking about Fanny, I tell him.

I know he finds the mention of Fanny irresistible. He has a story about her that he loves to tell, a story I've heard more than once, but I like the story, too; I know how it ends.

He clears his throat and begins.

Fanny was a purebred collie my father received for his fourth birthday. There was something wrong with her right front leg, and so she kept it tucked against her chest and hopped around on three paws. He has a picture of the two of them that he stores in an old tobacco tin with his other keepsakes, like the wallet my mother gave him on the day of their wedding that he carried until its seams split and the corners were worn round. In the photo, my father crouches next to Fanny. His arm is curved across her back. His body hides her bad leg and they squint into the distance, both looking faintly amused.

Fanny had been an adult dog when she became my father's pet. He liked to think they were the same age, growing up together. They had their routine: walks in the morning before he went to school, twilight games of fetch, fishing in Steven's Creek in the summer. Fanny liked to catch and eat crickets; she often brought my father a mangled offering in case he had a taste for insects himself. My father whispered the names of his crushes into Fanny's furry ear.

As the years passed, Fanny's joints stiffened, her limp became more pronounced and all around her muzzle, the fur turned white. Her eyes appeared sunken in their sockets. Sometimes she stood in the front yard, staring at the house, perplexed, as if she'd never seen it before. She lost her appetite. Settling herself to sleep, she whimpered in pain. She was suffering, my grandfather told my father.

On a Sunday, my father says, when he and Fanny were both ten, his daddy decided the time had come to put Fanny to sleep. My grandfather placed two cyanide capsules in the box that was Fanny's bed. Fanny jumped in the box and turned around a few times; my grandfather placed a board over the top of the box and said they needed to hurry or else they'd be late for church.

Of course my father never explains what he thought on their walk to church. They were Methodists; it was spring in Nebraska, so chances are the day was warm, sunny, dust on the road rising around their ankles. In the church, sunlight bled through stained glass, and the sermon, undoubtedly, was about salvation, eternal life, acceptance and suffering, damnation.

In some versions of this story, it's Easter Sunday. Tonight, it's only a Sunday in March.

Did my father listen to the minister, trying to find some words of comfort in the sermon? Did he stare out the window and wonder if, even at that moment, the cyanide capsules were dissolving in Fanny's mouth? Did he pray or simply remember afternoon walks with Fanny in the pasture behind their house, her first litter of puppies, the time she dragged a bloody rabbit inside during Thanksgiving dinner?

Home again after the service, my father followed his daddy to Fanny's bed.

In the telling of the story, he pauses. He stretches out this moment of suspense for maximum effect, even though we both know how the story ends. He looks up at Mars and makes his nightly comment: Closer than it's been in sixty thousand years!

Watching him gaze up at the sky, I imagine this must have been the position he adopted years ago and miles away, home from church on a Sunday that may or may not have been Easter. He wasn't going to look right away when his father lifted the board off Fanny's box. He was going to pretend for one more minute that she still lived.

And then the board was removed. The minute my father had allowed himself to pretend had barely begun when Fanny sprang out of the box. She licked my father's face; she danced around him on her three good legs, then trotted off to the old skillet that was her food dish. My grandfather, puzzled, searched through the bedding for the uneaten cyanide capsules, only to discover that they were gone. Apparently Fanny had consumed enough cyanide to kill a man, and it gave her a new lease on life.

My father always smiled when he got to that part of the story, and he turns to me now, smiling, holding out a yellow squash, a few green beans, knobby and fuzzed, a perfect gold tomato. Fanny lived three more years after the cyanide episode and died peacefully in her sleep. No one ever referred to her experience as a miracle, but I don't know what else to call it. Overhead, Mars shines through the branches of the neighbor's tree, so it looks like a lightning bug caught in a spider's web. I take the vegetables from my father. Even as we stand on earth made up from leaves and mulch and the bodies of animals, the golden planet slowly pulls away from us.

In the Field of Cement Animals

D ebbie and I were Irish twins. We'd been born in the same year, me in January, Debbie ten months later in November. Now that we were fourteen and thirteen, everyone thought Debbie was the oldest. She was taller, for one thing, and she had a certain confidence, a way of walking right into situations or groups of people without any of the gestures that signal fear—lowered eyes, nervous smoothings of clothes, the tentative smile. All my life, it seemed, I'd followed behind Debbie: she was the first to walk, the first to talk, the first one of us to stroll up to a boy, tilt her head and narrow her eyes in a way that made him swallow and step back.

The day I saw her render Tommy Wycoff almost mute, Mom and I had spent the morning canning tomatoes. Mason jars lining the counter glowed in sunlight. Peeled, the tomatoes were slippery as soapy dishes. Juice and seeds coated my hands and trailed along my forearms. Red strips of tomato skin were stuck to the sides of the sink.

"How about BLTs for lunch?" Mom asked.

"I'll have a BL," I said. "I've had enough of Ts today."

"Me, too." Mom screwed lids on a row of jars and used tongs to set them in the big kettle of boiling water that bubbled on the stove.

Working together like this invited confidences, and I was on the verge of telling her what I'd been noticing the past few weeks about Debbie. My sister had always been prone to illness—her allergies kicked up this time of year, then she usually caught a bad cold or strep throat after school started. Last Christmas she'd been hospitalized with pneumonia. At breakfast this morning, there were dark circles under her eyes, and Mom told her, "Deb, you look like you're coming down with something. You need to rest. Connie and I can take care of the tomatoes."

Debbie had nodded. In the bright morning light, her lips were pale, bloodless.

What I wanted to talk to Mom about was the way Debbie's vision had seemed a little off lately. Occasionally when I handed her something, her fingers would close over empty air a few inches to the left or right of what I held. Other times, when our bedroom was dark and I asked her a question, she'd looked toward the bed where I slept, even if I was hanging clothes in the closet or standing by the window, hoping for a breeze. Seeing her stare at the bed, nodding, as if someone were actually there, made the hair on my arms stand up. It was like watching a person talking to a ghost.

I slid two big whole tomatoes into a jar and packed them down. You had to cram them into the jar that way; the tomatoes shrank when they cooked in boiling water, and if they weren't packed tightly, you'd end up with jars that were half watery juice, half tomatoes.

"Mom?" I pressed two more tomatoes into the jar.

"Yes?"

I glanced out the window and saw Debbie walking across the back yard. She wore a dress, the one she'd gotten for Easter, and was carrying sandals in one hand. Sunlight shimmered off her long blond hair. She was headed east, toward the road that led past the big field of cement lawn ornaments where we'd played hide-and-seek when we were little. Automatically, my hand reached for another tomato. I could feel myself frowning. Where was she going, dressed up, when I was here working and she was supposed to be getting some rest? Normally I didn't resent Debbie being excused from chores, but the fact that she was sneaking off somewhere—that she hadn't at least included me by whispering her plans before she went upstairs—rubbed me the wrong way. Tomato juice stung in the little nicks left by the paring knife, steam rolling off the kettle had turned the kitchen air humid and sticky. If Debbie had been helping, we'd have finished hours ago. Watching her cross the lawn, I thought, *If she's well enough to get dressed up and go for a walk, then her blurry vision or whatever is wrong is probably nothing.* The words I'd decided on—*I think Debbie might need glasses*—were on the tip of my tongue, but I bit them back and said, "Do you want me to start the bacon when I'm done with this?"

"Sure," Mom said.

I didn't tell on Debbie, that she wasn't resting now, that there might be something wrong with her eyes. A breeze ruffled the hem of Debbie's dress and she disappeared around the corner of the house. *Loyalty,* I would have said right then, if Mom had asked my why I kept it all secret. *Respect for privacy.* But there were other reasons, I suppose. There always are.

I took a tray with a sandwich and a glass of lemonade up to our room for Debbie, who, of course, wasn't there. "She's sleeping," I told Mom when I went back downstairs. We ate lunch without talking; it was pleasant to sit quietly in the cool dining room, waiting for a breeze to blow through the screens.

"Maybe I'll take a nap," I said after I scraped the crusts into the trash. I wasn't sure how long I could conceal the fact that Debbie was gone—and that I'd lied about it, earlier. But when I stepped into our bedroom, she was sitting on her bed, eating the sandwich I'd left.

"Where have you been?"

She chewed and swallowed, looking right into my eyes. "What happened to the tomatoes? You left them off."

"We were sick of tomatoes since we've been canning them all morning." I sat down, hard, on my bed, making the springs creak. "I saw you in the backyard. Where'd you go?"

"I went to meet Tommy Wycoff in the cement animals field. He was supposed to be there at noon, but he didn't show up."

"Tommy Wycoff?" I knew Tommy Wycoff—at least, I knew who he *was*. That fall he'd be a senior at Langley High, four years ahead of Debbie and three years ahead of me. His family owned the grocery store in Langley and acres of land outside of town. He was handsome in a grown-up way, but he was so much older than we were, it was like Debbie had told me she'd arranged a rendezvous with one of our teachers. "Why were you meeting Tommy Wycoff?"

"I ran into him when Mom sent me to the grocery store yesterday, to get some lids for the Mason jars. He said he'd like to talk to me some more and I should meet him by the cement animals today."

I sat on the bed, blinking. Was Tommy Wycoff interested in my little sister?

"So let's go back this afternoon." Debbie rattled the ice in her lemonade. "Maybe he'll show up."

We explained to Mom that Debbie was feeling better, that we'd decided to take a walk, and left the house. Dust hovered above the road. Gravel pressed into the soles of my sneakers. Debbie hummed to herself, a tune I didn't recognize. Ahead, in their field, the cement animals stood stunned by the sunlight, their grey backs and shoulders the color of the road we walked on.

Before I was born, the cement animals were part of a lawn ornament business run by a man named Lloyd Triplett. These animals, along with some dinosaurs and statues of saints, were display figures. Eventually the business went bankrupt and Lloyd Triplett moved, leaving the figures behind. The Catholic Church adopted the saints for their courtyard, and the city moved the three dinosaurs to the park and painted them green. The animals, however, remained in their original spot, years of snow and hail, then blazing summers, barely pocking the cement skin of their backs. There was a yawning rhino, three lions standing with their heads raised, scenting the air, a bear with a fish caught in one his lifted paws. Two elephants, a mother and her baby, a Clydesdale stallion, a circus seal balancing a ball on his nose. The one I liked best was an enormous gorilla on his hind feet, arms raised, an ambiguous expression on his face that could be either greeting or threat. Every one of them was life-sized, cast in concrete, heavier than anything you could imagine. Winters, when snow covered the ground, each animal appeared lonely and distinct, but now, with the weeds growing up around them, they seemed to be members of a friendly but mismatched herd.

Debbie followed the overgrown driveway into the field. Grass brushed my knees. I squinted against the shimmering light. Then Tommy Wycoff stepped out from behind the mother elephant and leaned against her side. He wore a white t-shirt and jeans, smeared with streaks of grease. He folded his arms across his chest. "Hey, Deb." He looked at me and dipped his head.

Debbie walked right up to him. "I came here earlier," she said. "You said noon, didn't you?"

"Might have."

"You did." Debbie gazed into his face, hands on her hips. "You lied to me, already."

"Something came up."

"Like what?"

The air smelled of scorched grass. Sweat gathered along my hairline and in the crooks of my elbows. I wished I were home, sitting on the front porch with a glass of iced tea and a magazine.

"Like my dad sent me off to get a new alternator for the pickup and it took longer than it should of—"

"That's okay." Debbie's voice dropped from the shrill questioning tone to something lower. A hot breeze lifted her hair. She put her hand on Tommy's arm and gazed into his eyes. I didn't know how she could do it: the sun was behind his head, she must have been blinded by all that light. And she was only thirteen— who had showed her how to act this way? She and Tommy stood absolutely still. I saw his throat move when he swallowed, and then he looked down at her hand, at the spot where their skin touched.

For the two weeks we went to the field of cement animals to meet Tommy, every time seemed identical to the time before: Tommy's pickup parked at the back of the overgrown driveway, the sun blazing over head, or, if we went to the field after dinner, hanging lower in the sky like a balloon leaking air. Tommy stood behind one of the animals, smoking. He stepped out, said, "Hi, Connie, hi, Deb." We talked a little, then Debbie would reach for Tommy's hand, and they'd walk off into the weeds together.

A long, low building that had been Lloyd Triplett's office stood at the back of the field. The doors had been torn off their hinges and the two windows along the south wall had been broken so long ago that not even shards of glass in the corners of the frames remained. Inside the building, a few small cement figurines lay tipped on their sides or hidden in corners. While Tommy and Debbie were off in the field, I explored the building, slowly, making myself focus on each detail to have something to do. I collected the lawn ornaments I found and set them in the middle of the room: two turtles, a gargoyle, a rabbit, a tiny baby duck that must have been one of several molded to follow after a mother duck. A few of the ornaments were chipped, but not badly, and I decided I'd take them home, one by one, a reward to myself for waiting around while Tommy and Debbie did whatever it was they did.

On the walks home, Debbie's cheeks were flushed. The skin around her mouth looked pink. Sometimes I reached over and removed a piece of grass from her hair. We'd hurry up the stairs to our room, and I'd hide whatever ornament I'd brought home in the closet. Debbie went into the bathroom, washed her face, and came out looking the way she always looked, unkissed. At night, lying in bed, I asked her what she and Tommy did when they went off into the grass.

"We talk," she said. I could hear Dad in the bathroom, running water. We kept our voices low. "We kiss, you know. He want to—he wants—" she cleared her throat. "To do other things. Take off my shirt."

Outside, cicadas buzzed in the trees. The breeze that came through the screen held the slightest touch of coolness. Floorboards creaked under Dad's feet when he moved down the hall. I thought I should have been the one telling Debbie's story, since I was older. I should have been the one to experience things first, explain them to my little sister, conscious of her in the bed a few feet away from mine, propped against the pillows, listening, waiting for my next words. *This is what it's like, but you have to be careful, you can't believe everything a boy might say to you.* I said, "Be careful," and I sounded exactly the way Mom did when she watched us use sharp knives.

"Connie," Debbie said, and I waited for her to continue, but she got up and went into the bathroom, and by the time she got back, I was almost asleep.

The first day of the county fair, Debbie and I got up early. We showered and dressed in floral skirts we'd made a few years before for 4-H projects. Debbie's hem was a little crooked because she'd only pinned it, not basted it the way you were supposed to. But on Debbie, a crooked hem wasn't something you'd notice.

The fairgrounds sat on the outskirts of town, three big metal Quonset huts and a barn for the animals. Fields of wheat waved on either side of the road. The car's tires churned up dust. In the backseat, Debbie sneezed and sneezed. Mom glanced in the rearview mirror. "Did you take your allergy pills this morning?"

"Yes. Of course."

We parked and crossed the gravel lot to the Quonset hut where, two days earlier, we'd left our entries for judging. Then, the hut had been a mess of contestants' boxed entries, floor gritty with dust, the women writing out tags looking sweaty and tired. Today, the cement felt swept and smooth under my feet. White butcher paper covered long tables, with the different classes of items arranged on top. Canned goods gleamed in sunlight. Carefully folded quilts hung on racks behind the tables, ribbons dangling from some of them. Pies and plates of cookies sat in straight rows. Framed paintings lined the Quonset's back wall. Debbie had made some strawberry jam and a pink halter top. She got a red, second-prize ribbon on the jam, nothing on the halter. We walked up and down the aisles, talking to people we knew, admiring a tiny set of doll clothes, a lavender wool jacket with silver buttons, searching for the crocheted tablecloth Mom had been working on all year, the baby blanket I'd knitted, my jar of tomatoes.

"That's too bad about the halter top," I said to Debbie. "I thought it was cute."

Debbie shrugged. "I don't care."

A horse neighed from the barn. A little boy in overalls led a sheep past the windows. I spotted Mom's tablecloth, a blue ribbon attached to its entry tag. "Look!" The baby blanket had gotten a red ribbon, and I felt my heart clutch with disappointment. Only second prize. I rubbed my fingers over the slick ribbon.

"Sweetie," Mom said. "There's a lot of entries in that category. Lots of things that didn't win a prize at all."

"I know."

"Let's find your tomatoes."

The tomatoes made up for the baby blanket—a purple ribbon, *first prize*, gleamed against the jar. "Good job, Connie!" Mom squeezed my arm.

I waited for Debbie to say something, but she was looking toward the door. A shadow fell into the room, followed by the body that cast it: Tommy Wycoff. "Oh, Tommy Wycoff's here," Debbie said. Her voice was as casual as if she'd noticed our neighbor, Mrs. Peters, or one of the teachers from school. "I think I'll go over and say hi."

"That's fine." Mom sounded distracted; she was looking at the other jars of tomatoes, the ones I'd beaten. "You really did a good job with yours," she told me. "I know some of these belong to people who've been canning for years."

"Mm." I watched Debbie approach Tommy. His face transformed when he saw her. His head lifted, he smiled, the corners of his eyes turning up. A person couldn't stop herself from thinking how handsome he was. Tommy spoke, and Debbie nodded. She left him standing by a table covered with cookies and pies and came back over to us. "Is it okay if I go over to the sheep judging?" she asked Mom.

Mom looked at her, and then across the room at Tommy. "Well, all right. For a little while." Debbie and Tommy moved through the Quonset's door and into the sunlight. Mom sighed. "Now who is that boy?"

"Tommy Wycoff."

"That's right. He's the nephew of the man with the lawn ornament business." Mom was still staring at the door. "He's a little older than you girls, isn't he?"

I swallowed. Tommy Wycoff was seventeen, old enough to drive, almost old enough to vote. If Mom knew exactly how old Tommy was, she'd probably want to go after Debbie, snatch her back, and I supposed there would be a little scene in the livestock judging arena, Debbie's voice going shrill: *But you said all right—!* "Oh, a little older," I said.

Mom sighed again. "I was hoping Debbie would wait awhile before she started being interested in boys."

Did she mean, wait until after a boy had showed some interest in me? In our town, siblings were often identified by a particular trait—*the lazy one,* or *the redhead.* Debbie and I were still young enough to be distinguished by our birth order, but I imagined that a few years down the road, Debbie would become—what? *The pretty one? The wild sister?* And I'd be known as a *Good girl*, or, worse, *Mannerly but plain*. Looking down at my jar of tomatoes, I felt as if my whole summer had been wasted on useless projects, an accumulation of objects that I'd created for no real purpose. I'd donate the baby blanket to the church for its Christmas basket campaign, we'd eat the purple-ribbon tomatoes that would taste no different from all the other tomatoes at home. And the ribbons themselves were poor mementos, nothing like pictures: they wouldn't help me remember what these things looked like, what they'd meant to me while I was making them.

It was always the same: Tommy's pickup parked at the back of the driveway, the weeds in the field no taller or shorter than the time before. I walked around the office building, collecting the abandoned ornaments. At home, Debbie and I called hello to our parents and hurried upstairs. Debbie washed her face; I hid whatever ornament I'd brought home on the floor of our closet, back in the corner. Years later, the day before I got married, when I was taking my clothes and shoes out of the closet to pack in boxes, my fingers brushed one of the turtles and I sat back on my heels. *What on earth?* Debbie sat on her bed. By then, she could only see shadows. I took the whole collection of ornaments out of the closet and arranged them around her on the mattress. Even after all these years, I could remember the order in which I'd brought them home, the baby duck first, then the gargoyle, then the two turtles, which were the heaviest. "Here," I said, and set the baby duck in her lap. She stroked her fingers over his cement back, his little beak.

"A bird?" she guessed.

"Right."

She reached out and touched the other ornaments, one by one. "They were in the closet?"

"That summer, you know," I said. "The summer you first got sick, when we'd go to the field where the cement animals are—I brought them home then."

"Oh." She lifted one of the turtles, pressing her fingers into the spot where his shell was chipped. "That summer Tommy Wycoff was there."

I nodded, then realized she couldn't see the gesture. "Yes, that summer."

A week after the fair, school started. On the second day, Debbie fainted in the hallway between classes. My parents were called to come to the nurse's office, and I sat next to them on a hard wooden chair whose varnish had turned sticky in the heat. A ceiling fan turned tiredly above our heads. The nurse stepped out of an adjoining room and shut the door behind her. "She's resting right now." She pulled up a chair and sat facing us. "I think you need to take Debbie in for some tests. She's fifteen pounds lighter than last year. That's not normal for a girl her age."

My father pressed his lips together and looked down at his hands. Mom was holding her purse on her lap, and she lifted it up and then set it down again. For some reason, they looked at me.

"Debbie doesn't—" The nurse cleared her throat. "Debbie doesn't make herself vomit after she eats, does she?"

"No," I said. "No, but—" They waited, heads tilted warily. I realized I should have said something sooner, weeks ago. "It seems like there might be something wrong with her eyes."

"Eyes?" the nurse prompted.

"The past few days," I said, though it had been longer than that. "It seems like she can't see very well."

The nurse nodded. She appeared relieved by this information. "Maybe Debbie needs glasses. You know sometimes vision impairments can bring on headaches, and that might have caused Debbie to faint."

"But the weight loss," Mom said.

The nurse nodded, opened her mouth to speak, and then remained silent.

Later that week, Mom and Dad drove Debbie to Madison for tests. I had school; I had to stay behind. All day I kept looking up at the clock, trying to imagine exactly what they were doing. Was Debbie on a raised hospital bed, her arm stretched out for a nurse to insert a needle and draw blood? Were Mom and Dad standing next to her, or waiting outside the room? Maybe the tests were over quickly, and they were having lunch now, or even shopping. Maybe they were already home.

"Well, we were lucky," Mom said that night at dinner. She'd made a roast. I watched Dad carve the meat. Debbie was upstairs, sleeping. She'd been in bed since they'd gotten back from Madison, sleeping or pretending to sleep whenever I was in the room, not responding when I whispered her name. "The tests came back, and even if the results aren't what we'd hoped—"

"She's diabetic," my father said. He set the knife, carefully, against the plate. "She'll have to take insulin for the rest of her life."

I'd heard of insulin, and I thought it involved needles. "You mean, she'll have to get shots?"

"She'll have to learn how to give herself shots. And she's going to have to take it easy, watch what she eats." He handed me the platter with the sliced roast on it. Potatoes and carrots arranged around the meat rolled together as I took it; I realized my hands were shaking. *Debbie was really sick.*

"Does she know?"

Mom nodded. "She's upset, you know—"

"I know," I said.

"But it could have been worse. If she hadn't fainted, we wouldn't have had the tests done, and there's a chance—" Mom lifted her napkin to her mouth, suddenly. Her eyes filled. I looked down at my plate. I'd never seen either of my parents cry, or even close. "There's a chance she could have just suddenly gone into a coma. This way, at least, we can take care of her."

"Of course," I said.

"Connie, it was so good you noticed that her vision was blurry—that's one of the symptoms."

What if I'd said something sooner? I wanted to ask, to have the answer absolve me, but I knew the truth could go the other way, too. As it was, Debbie's diagnosis and treatment occurred before anything terrible happened. By fainting, she'd been the one who offered up the clue, not me—even though I'd known for weeks that she wasn't seeing very well. But I'd kept this information to myself, along with the nightly meetings with Tommy Wycoff, as if the two were connected. The blindness, the boy. I swallowed and looked down at my plate, at the slices of meat and bright orange carrots. Mom reached across the table and patted my hand, giving me comfort when I should have been scolded, sent to bed without supper. Forced, even, to hear the words: *You're jealous, aren't you? That's why you kept it secret?*

Early evening, the day before Debbie fainted, the day before everything changed, Debbie and I went to the field to meet Tommy. The sky had faded to a pale, washed-out blue and the sun hovered above the horizon, a ball of fire. We stomped down the weeds around the gorilla and sat on the ground, resting our backs against his legs, Tommy and Debbie against one leg, me against the other. Tommy had his arm over Debbie's shoulders. He talked about his classes, how people had changed over the summer, a fat girl becoming so thin in only three months that he didn't recognize her at first.

Did Debbie not like listening to him talk about another girl? She stood up, suddenly, and brushed off the seat of her shorts. "Let's play hide-and-seek," she said. "Tommy's it."

He looked up at her. "Deb, that's kid stuff."

"I don't care. Count to twenty, and Connie and I will hide."

"Deb—"

"Count," she said. "Cover your eyes. Don't cheat."

Tommy sighed, but did what she said. Debbie and I moved off into the field together, then separated. I went to the office and sat on the floor by the remaining ornaments, the ones I hadn't brought home yet. I figured Tommy would find Debbie first, he'd press her back, laughing, against whatever animal she'd hidden behind, no thought of anything but my sister in his head. I pushed one turtle closer to the other turtle. Its base scraped against the floor, and, seconds later, Tommy poked his head in the door. "Caught you," he said. He kept his eyes on mine and stepped into the building. How did Debbie feel when he looked at her this way? Did she grow conscious of her blood pulsing in her wrists and behind her ears, a sensation that made me, finally, turn my head away? "I haven't been inside this place in years."

"My mother said Lloyd Triplett was your uncle," I told him, standing.

"Yeah. Great uncle, actually."

I picked up one of the turtles, and we went out into the field, searching for Debbie.

The sun was halfway concealed by the horizon. For twenty minutes, Tommy and I stumbled around the field, catching our feet on big clumps of crabgrass. "Debbie!" he yelled. "We give up!" We waited for her reply. Cicadas hummed in the trees that circled the field and tall weeds rattled when the breeze pushed them together.

"Jesus, she's stubborn," Tommy said. A streak of dirt bisected his cheek. What would happen if I reached out to wipe it away? What would such boldness feel like? But Tommy belonged to Debbie. I kept my hands to myself.

"Debbie!" Her name filled the field. "I'm leaving," he yelled, as if that would make her appear. I knew she wouldn't come out from wherever she was. That would be breaking the rule of hide and seek, the rule that we were supposed to look until we found her, and not give up.

"I've got to go," Tommy said. "Tell her I'll see her tomorrow."

"All right."

I watched Tommy jog along the pitted driveway to his truck. The engine growled. His arm came out the driver's window to wave, and the brake lights winked twice. Then he was gone, dust rolling in the air behind him. He left then, and a few weeks later, after we'd found out about Debbie's diabetes, Tommy was never in the field when we went there after supper. Maybe the needles scared him. The day he'd paid an actual visit to the house and the three of us sat on the porch, Debbie lifted up her shirt and injected insulin into the skin of her abdomen, right in front of him. Maybe it was the words *chronic illness*, all the risks that might be lying in wait, her new thick glasses. People in town had started referring to her as *the sick one*, their voices grave. Tommy might have told himself he was doing the right thing. After all, she was only thirteen and he was four years older. It was the kind of situation that could get you in trouble with the law. He might have thought, *I came to my senses! I did it for her!* I don't suppose Tommy thinks about Debbie now at all.

Standing alone in the field after Tommy left, I yelled, "Debbie!" The land was so flat my voice didn't echo a bit. "Debbie!" My throat felt raw from screaming. Methodically, I circled the animals closest to me, the bear, the seal. The setting sun turned his ball into a globe of fire.

When Debbie was little, she'd silently travel from one hiding place to another, so spots I'd already looked had to be checked again, over and over. I moved through the weeds, as quietly as possible, listening hard for any sound of movement. We needed to get home soon, or Mom and Dad would worry.

She wasn't by the Clydesdale, or the lions, or the baby elephant. Hours seemed to have passed before I finally found her. She stood behind the mother elephant's back leg, a shadow. At last, I heard her breathing, a little click in her throat each time she inhaled. "Connie?" she said when I touched her arm. The sun had set. Dusk surrounded us. All over the field, the animals stood quietly, their weight holding the earth in place. It was so dark I could barely see.

Comanche's Story

What the horse saw before collapsing, arrow-shot and stunned, too far from the river to drink:

One minute Custer's Seventh Calvary marched in formation toward the Little Bighorn, Comanche bearing the familiar weight of his master, Captain Keogh. Sun overhead, grass underfoot, locusts singing in the weeds. The next minute, Indians screamed down from the bluff. More howled up behind. The Seventh Calvary found themselves surrounded, surprised. The Indians besieged them with arrows, muskets, rifles, knives. Horses stampeded, blood burst from wounds. Indians dragged Keogh off Comanche's back and bludgeoned him. Dirt everywhere, and blood. So much noise the locusts went silent. Desperate soldiers shot their mounts and stacked the still-warm bodies as if that wall of flesh could save them.

All that sacrifice came down to one living creature left in the Seventh Cavalry: this horse. Everything was hushed, all dead, but him.

He lay, blinking away flies, smelling the water of the river, longing to stand and drink. At last more soldiers came to bury the dead. Seeing the horse alive moved some of them to tears. They gave Comanche water, dressed his wounds. A hero, he was sent to live in leisure at Fort Lincoln, where he poached sugar cubes from officers, gravely drank his daily bucket of beer.

He'd seen the one who killed Custer; he knew the answer to

the question that would plague historians, forever. Historians, the curious, those who wanted to assign reverence or blame. They came to touch him, to stare into his eyes and croon, *Tell me what you saw.*

Oh, he remembered what he'd seen, the screaming men, the blood, the way his own kind jerked from bullets; when they fell, their bodies thumped up clouds of dust. If he could speak, what would he say in answer to their question? Perhaps, *White Bull shot Custer.* Or *It was Gall.* Or would he tell them, *Does it matter, after all? Dead is dead.*

Comanche let his visitors stroke the scars that marred his fine coat, trace the divots left from arrows, as if they were blind and his skin the Braille they touched to find the answers that they needed. "So gentle," they said, feeling only a puff of breath against their hands, a whiskery stroke of lip; his teeth never touched flesh when he took the offerings they brought—carrots, sugar cubes, the apples that were sweeter in the places bruised.

Strange and Dangerous Things

No one knew how deep the creek was. It meandered through the farm Annabelle's grandparents owned, curling past the ravine filled with junked cars and snaking, acres away, behind the barn. There, the creek rose all the way up the grassy banks, its water the muddy color of fish so you couldn't see the bottom, which could have been inches or yards—or even miles—below the surface. Clearly the creek posed a danger for someone who couldn't swim very well. She might not be able to touch bottom; the current might sweep her away. Annabelle knew, after all, that you could drown on two tablespoons of water ingested the wrong way. It was a scientific fact.

On Saturdays, Annabelle's father took Annabelle and her little sister Karen to the farm, which was in Eagle, twenty miles from Lincoln. Annabelle's mother never joined them on these excursions. She said she was allergic to the wildflowers that covered the old wheat field; allergic to the farm dogs; bored out of her skull with the conversations between Annabelle's father and his sisters. Annabelle liked the farm, and she liked the fact her mother didn't come along. Her mother had a lot of rules that Annabelle's father forgot about when she wasn't there to remind him. For instance, he didn't care what they did on the farm, as long as they didn't go near the creek; he didn't care how dirty they got. He never made them wash their hands after they petted the dogs.

Annabelle especially treasured the dogs, since she wasn't

permitted one of her own. There were two—Lady, a drool-y collie mix, and small, silent Babe, everyone's favorite, part Pug and part terrier, who had the markings of a Holstein cow.

On the Saturday after Annabelle had lost her last baby tooth and gained the ability—suddenly, miraculously—to read, her father even let the girls stand up on the car's back seat once he'd turned onto the gravel road that ended at the farm. Standing on the seat! Annabelle marveled, her hands pressed against the car's roof to keep her balance. The week had been full of milestones, though Annabelle's ability to read had actually driven a little wedge between her and her father.

Ever since she was a baby, he read to her for a half-hour every evening—fairy tales; old Horatio Alger books he'd had as a boy; an occasional Nancy Drew mystery. They'd been reading "The Little Mermaid" on Monday night, and her father had stopped halfway through the story because it was time for Annabelle to go to bed.

Annabelle hated stopping in the middle of stories. She wanted to know how things ended. All the elements of the mermaid's life had been set before her—the beautiful underwater world, the mermaid's longing to see the world above. When the mermaid turned fifteen and was going to be allowed to rise to the surface of the sea, her grandmother snapped oysters along her tail as decorations. The shells pinched, and the little mermaid complained.

Above the sea, the little mermaid saved a handsome prince when a storm destroyed his ship. She fell in love with him, and she longed to become human like he was so they could marry. That transformation required the assistance of a witch, who demanded payment for a potion that would turn the mermaid's tail into the stumpy appendages that humans called legs.

Listening to the story, Annabelle stretched her legs out straight. How would it feel to have a tail instead of limbs? She pressed her legs tight against each other and put her heels together with her feet pointed out to look like fins.

Her father paused in his reading. One of Annabelle's back molars was loose—her last remaining baby tooth—and she wobbled it with her index finger, just until she heard the faint tearing sound her gums made before things really started to hurt. She removed her finger from her mouth and waited. "So the witch told the little mermaid she wanted the oysters clamped on her tail, since they were full of pearls," her father read.

Annabelle was glad to hear the mermaid was relieved from her torment of decoration. "And now it's time for bed," her father said.

The next day after school, Annabelle picked up the Hans Christian Anderson book. She was in second grade, and in reading class they'd been studying the adventures of Dick and Jane, which were related in large letters and short sentences and accompanied by informative pictures that nudged you to understand, for instance, that the question Dick was asking might concern the cake that Mother held.

Annabelle was comfortable with big letters and short sentences. She normally found small print and dense paragraphs intimidating and not worth the trouble it took to decipher all those long and unfamiliar words. But this afternoon, a switch in her brain must have moved to the *on* position, because she found herself scanning the first paragraph of the story her father had read the night before with perfect ease.

Far out in the ocean, where the water is as blue as the prettiest cornflower, and as clear as crystal, it is very, very deep; so deep, indeed, that no cable could fathom it.

She remembered the word *fathom* from the previous evening. She slid onto the couch and continued reading, repeating the part she'd already heard, some of which turned out to be different than what her father had related. For one thing, the mermaid didn't give the witch the pinching oysters in payment for the potion.

Instead, the witch cut out the little mermaid's tongue so that the witch would acquire her beautiful voice.

Cut out her tongue! So the little mermaid was mute.

Annabelle scowled. She wondered, momentarily, what had caused her father to make up this part—to *lie*—but she wanted to find out what happened, and so she turned back to the book.

That night, her father settled into the couch and patted the cushion. "Ready for some more 'Little Mermaid'?"

Annabelle sat next to him. She took the book from his hand and held it on her lap. "I already finished it."

"You finished reading it? Yourself?"

Annabelle nodded. "This afternoon. You know the witch cut out her tongue."

Her father was silent for a moment. "Well, yes, I did know that," he said. He got up and went into the family room, and Annabelle heard the television boom to life. Holding the book, she felt an odd sensation sloshing around in her chest that she would, years later, identify as guilt.

That week, Annabelle spent most of her free time pouring over her mother's *Good Housekeeping* magazine. She felt as though she'd stumbled upon a vast valuable mound of information she couldn't quite make sense of. There were puzzling advertisements: stories about people who'd been fat, but then discovered a miraculous candy you consumed before a meal and it cut your appetite in half, so the pounds just fell away. Annabelle examined the "before" pictures of women in tent-like dresses, their exposed upper arms the size of hams; then, the "after" pictures that showed women half the size they'd been. Half the size! They'd lost the weight of an entire person.

The ads Annabelle found even more compelling were for Clairol haircolor. The mysterious and somewhat ominous headline made Annabelle's brain spin with curiosity: *Only her hairdresser knows for sure.*

Knows *what*? Annabelle rocked her loose tooth with her tongue, thinking.

She could ask her mother, but she suspected the question might result in the magazine's confiscation. And she wanted to read the column called "My Problem and How I Solved It." This month's subtitle claimed, "My husband's brother was a funny uncle."

A funny uncle, Annabelle said to herself. Did that mean he was like Red Skelton? She hid behind the couch in the family room and read the article, which took her two hours and left her bleary-eyed, anxious, her head filled with new facts, new information about the world and all the strange and dangerous things that filled it. The next morning, her tooth fell painlessly out of her mouth when she tapped it with her tongue.

On the farm, Annabelle, Karen, and Babe the dog spent the morning playing with a family of toads that lived in the window well beneath the screened-in porch where Annabelle's father sat with his two sisters. The grownups did what they always did when they were together: smoked cigarettes, slapped at buzzing flies with rolled-up kitchen towels, and carried on a conversation about other relatives, filled with mysterious references to *alcoholics, hysterectomies*, and *bankruptcy.*

Today they were talking about their Aunt Virginia, Grandma's older sister, who'd been Babe's mistress. Annabelle captured one of the baby toads and showed it to Babe, who wagged her tail and smiled up at Annabelle. In Annabelle's hands, the toad's skin felt cool and pebbled. Its sides swelled as it breathed and its funny toad eyes stared straight ahead.

Her father and his sisters related the various episodes of Aunt Virginia's life. When she was a young woman, she'd left Nebraska for the bright lights of Chicago and worked, for years, at Marshall Fields.

Annabelle handed the baby toad to her sister and reached for one of the bigger ones.

In Virginia's old age, she moved to a log cabin at the end of a dirt road somewhere in Missouri.

"Outside Sedalia, wasn't it?" Annabelle's father asked.

"That's right," Aunt Mary said.

The cabin had no indoor plumbing, no electricity, and no address. Annabelle's father related these details in a tone of admiration.

"And she owned a shotgun, don't forget that," Aunt Mary said.

"A shotgun and Babe for protection." Annabelle's father chuckled.

"Babe wasn't much protection. Since she never barks."

Annabelle's father inhaled on his cigarette. "Where is Babe, anyway?"

"I think she's with the girls."

Aunt Virginia also liked to dress in her dead brother Guy's World War I uniform. In fact, that's what she'd been wearing when she died, Aunt Janet informed them in a whisper.

Annabelle caught the larger toad. It struggled in her hands, and so she put it back in the window well and looked around for something they might like to eat.

"Grass?" her sister suggested.

Aunt Mary said, "I'd bet money she was a lesbian."

Annabelle had been breaking off pieces of grass when she heard the word *lesbian*. A new word, one she'd never heard spoken before, never yet seen in print. What did it mean?

Annabelle looked at Babe. Babe must know, on a level beyond speech, what that word signified, since the dog had spent her whole life with Aunt Virginia, had been with her every moment of every day until Aunt Virginia died and Babe, orphaned, came to live on the farm. *Lesbian*, Annabelle mouthed as she stared into Babe's eyes. The dog's curled tail wagged in a slightly jerky motion that reminded Annabelle of a mechanical toy.

After lunch, Annabelle's father announced that he was going to teach the girls to fish. Annabelle's heart sank. She hated fish. Nights when her mother served strips of cod baked with tomatoes and onions, she pushed the terrible food around on her plate, afraid to put any of the gummy filet in her mouth. Besides, she'd wanted to spend the afternoon exploring the old henhouse, which was filled with fascinating odds and ends: ancient catalogues, bent spoons, twine, tins that had once held tobacco. But her father seemed pleased with his fishing idea, and so she and Karen stood patiently while he sprayed them with 6-12, the bug spray that had a sick, waxy smell.

Armed with a pair of bamboo fishing poles, a shovel, a length of clothesline, and a pail, her father led them to the garden, where he dug a shovelful of dirt squirming with worms and dumped it in the pail. Annabelle was handed a fishing pole to carry; Karen was given the clothesline. They set off through the waist-high grass behind the barn. The fingers of a pair of gloves protruded from her father's back pocket and flapped as if waving as he walked. Birds drifted in the sky above them; bugs sang in the weeds.

Maybe, Annabelle thought, the act of fishing wouldn't be as bad as *eating* fish.

Her father chose a place where trees, growing along the creek's bank, cast a line of shade. The creek itself lay flat and mud-colored in the sun. Dragonflies hovered above the water. Anything could be under the surface, Annabelle thought—whole unknown kingdoms, whole families of mermaids.

"Get away from the edge," her father ordered. "You'll drown."

He measured out two lengths of clothesline and sawed the rope with his pocketknife.

"Come here," he said to Karen. He tied clothesline around her waist, making a u-shaped knot in the back where she couldn't turn around and untie it. Everyone in the family knew Karen had a strong aversion to restraint. As a baby, she'd smashed the bridge of her nose on the bars of her crib when she tried to escape, and her first word had been *Down!* "Hold this," he said and handed Karen a fishing pole.

And old elm stood some yards behind Karen, and their father—leaving her standing a safe distance from the water, but close enough to fish—looped the other end of the clothesline around the tree. "There," he said, satisfied, brushing his hands together.

Then he tied the other piece of rope around Annabelle's waist. "Too tight?"

"No."

Annabelle was attached to her own tree and given her own fishing pole to hold while their father returned to Karen. The rope, he explained, was for their own protection, like a seatbelt. It would keep them a safe distance from the water; it would keep them from falling in and going under. One kid you could keep an eye on, but two? What if Annabelle fell in, he went to save her, and then Karen fell in, too far away for him to reach?

He explained this while he baited Karen's hook. Annabelle had to look away from the worm that twisted as it was impaled. Lady and Babe pushed through the weeds.

"Don't fall in!" Karen said.

"The dogs know how to *swim*." Their father dumped out the dirt and took the pail to the edge of the creek to fill with water. "When you catch your fish, we'll put them in here."

Babe sat next to Annabelle. Her pink tongue fluttered as she panted. Annabelle's father approached, holding out a worm. "Do you want to put it on the hook?"

"No."

He cast their lines, told them to watch the bobbers resting on the water, and then leaned back against his own tree, a few feet behind them, and lit a cigarette.

Annabelle stood, holding the bamboo pole. So this was fishing: tied in place, sweating, waiting for something that might or might not happen. The smell from her father's Zippo lighter lingered in the air. She stared at the bobber, a blood-red dome floating on the water, and thought about the conversation she'd had that morning with her mother.

Before they'd left for the farm, Annabelle—overcome with curiosity about the Clairol ad—took the magazine into the kitchen. Her mother was spooning crystals from a small box into a juice glass. Annabelle tilted her head to read the lettering on the side of the box: KNOX GELATIN.

Her mother added water to the glass and stirred. She glared at the cloudy liquid, lifted the glass to her mouth, and drank.

"Mother," Annabelle said. She held out the magazine. "*What* does the hairdresser know?"

Her mother continued gulping the liquid. When she finished, she tapped the glass down on the counter and grimaced. "Christ, that tastes horrible."

"Why did you drink it?"

"It makes your fingernails grow." Her mother flexed her hands like a cat kneading its paws into a cushion. Her fingernails were long and almond-shaped, painted a frosty pink, and objects of envy to Annabelle, who was a nail-chewer.

A magic potion, Annabelle thought. Like the one the witch had given the little mermaid to allow her to grow legs. "Can I have some?"

"No. You're not old enough."

Annabelle rattled the magazine. "Mom. What does it mean that 'only her hairdresser knows for sure'? Knows *what*?"

Her mother glanced down at the ad. A sour expression remained on her face. "I don't know, Annabelle." She rinsed the glass out and set it in the dish drainer.

Her mother *did* know, Annabelle was sure. It must be something that Annabelle wasn't old enough to hear; it probably had something to do with the box that Annabelle had recently begun noticing in the bathroom, a box that appeared, remained for several days, and then vanished. It was a shade of purple that Annabelle found particularly appealing, and a lighter-colored rose bloomed in the box's center. On the front were the words KOTEX Sanitary Napkins. Inside the box—the most recent box—were long pads of cotton that Annabelle thought would make excellent mattresses for dolls' beds.

Soon she would ask about the purpose of those pads. She'd taken one and hidden it under her pillow, and she planned a confrontation when her mother came to tuck her into bed.

Possibly even tonight, Annabelle thought, staring sleepily at the bobber. She heard her father lighting another cigarette. Suddenly, the pole twitched against her fingers. The bobber sank below the water's surface and the pole's tip bent. She didn't know what to do. "It's moving," she said.

"What?"

"The pole is moving."

Annabelle's father crashed through the grass. Lady barked. The pole lurched in Annabelle's hands and dimples scattered across the surface of the creek.

"Don't drop it," Annabelle's father said. He reached for the pole, gave it a hard jerk, and lifted a thrashing fish from the water. "Look what you caught! A catfish!"

Karen came as close as her rope would allow to get a better look. The catfish—gray as the creek's water, with thick whiskers like tentacles—twisted in the air. A horrible croak rose from its mouth, like a toad being choked. Annabelle and Karen looked at each other.

Their father swung the fish over the grass. He pulled on his gloves, then dislodged the hook from the fish's mouth and dropped it into the pail. Back in water, the fish was silent. Their father stood over it, considering. "That's got to be nine inches long," he said. "Quite a catch, for your first fish."

Annabelle nodded.

"I'll cook it up right away," her father said. "There's nothing better than fresh fish."

Annabelle and Karen were untied. They followed their father back to the barn, where he propped the fishing poles against the wall. He carried the pail with him as he wandered around, looking for something.

"Can I go?" Karen asked.

"That's fine."

Enviously, Annabelle watched her sister run off toward the corn crib. How unfair it seemed that she, Annabelle, who had actually accomplished the goal of fishing had to remain bound to the project when there were other, more interesting, things to do.

In one corner of the barn, Annabelle's father located an old cutting board, a hammer, and a giant spike of a nail. He handed Annabelle the cutting board, which she tucked under her arm like a book, and they went back out into the streaming sunlight of early afternoon.

Outside, he motioned for Annabelle to give him the cutting board. He placed it on the ground. Babe and Annabelle watched her father kneel and position the fish—which was still alive and thrashing, but with less energy—in the middle of the board. The fish glared at them with its bulgy eyes, its whiskers twitching. It emitted another hoarse croak. Babe's ears swiveled at the sound.

"I'll clean this one, so you can see how it's done." Annabelle's father began hammering the nail through the fish's head, securing it to the board. At every stroke of the hammer, the fish slapped its tail against the wood. Annabelle felt the hammering take over the beat of her own heart, as if the tool were pounding into *her.* She gazed up at the sun until she was afraid she might go blind, and when she looked back, the fish was limp.

Cleaning a fish, her father explained, was easy enough: you cut open the stomach side, pulled out the innards, then sliced the opposite side to remove the spine. He sawed away with his pocket knife. Blood oozed from the fish, and Annabelle stepped back. She'd expected the fish to be filled with something else—creek water, maybe—not blood as red as her own that she'd seen pooling in the hole in her mouth after her tooth had fallen out.

A few barn cats joined them, lured by the smell.

Next, Annabelle's father showed how the fish's skin peeled off easily as a person's own sunburned skin after it blistered. The fins, he explained, were sharp, so you had to be careful. It was a good idea to wear gloves.

The cats fought each other over the strips of skin he tossed in the grass.

The last step involved slicing off the fish's head. Using the hammer's claws, Annabelle's father then pried the decapitated head off the board. He handed Annabelle the slippery fillets to hold and said, "Now comes the best part: cooking and eating."

Eating sounded like the worst part of fishing, even more awful than watching the fish's head nailed to the board. Glumly, Annabelle followed her father to the house.

In the kitchen, the aunts gathered around as her father explained how Annabelle had caught the fish all by herself—which wasn't exactly true, since he'd been the one to actually jerk the fish out of the water. He said it had been a huge fish, nearly twelve inches head to tail. The aunts nodded, impressed.

"Watch this," Annabelle's father instructed. He dipped the fish in milk and swished it around in a bowl of cornmeal. Then he set it in a cast-iron pan, shiny with bacon grease saved from the morning's breakfast.

The fish popped and hissed. The aunts smiled at Annabelle. "Hope you're hungry," Aunt Mary said.

"I can share," Annabelle said. "There's enough for everyone to have some."

Her father chuckled. He rested one hand on top of her head. With the other, he prodded a spatula against the fish. "No,

Annabelle, this is *your* fish. You caught it yourself, and there's no reason you have to share. You can eat the whole thing!"

Outside the kitchen window, sunlight radiated a melancholy end-of-the-afternoon quality. Across the table, Annabelle's father regarded her proudly. In front of her lay the lone object on a china plate: the fish.

Staring at the plate, Annabelle knew the time for protest had passed. She should have said something hours ago, said *no* when her father uttered the word *fishing*. She should have hooked the worm herself, cut her thumb open and allowed a bloody injury to provide distraction. She should have thrown up or fainted in a heap when she watched him clean the catfish.

Now, she had no choice.

She began to eat, knocking off flakes of the pale flesh with her fork and washing them down with mouthfuls of milk. In truth, it wasn't as bad as the fish her mother served, those filets extracted from boxes and frozen solid in a brick. This fish—Annabelle's fish—had a milder flavor, and the bacon grease obscured some of the taste, but still: it was fish.

When Aunt Mary called Annabelle's father into the living room to have a look at something, Annabelle fed clumps of catfish to Babe, who'd remained loyally by her side. Annabelle offered another forkful to the dog when her father went to the refrigerator to refill her glass with milk. Whenever she discovered one of the sharp, skinny bones that had been one of the fish's ribs or part of his spine, Annabelle made sure to keep them padded in as much flesh as possible when she pushed them aside. Even so, there was a lot of fish to eat.

"I'm full," Annabelle said finally. "I can't eat any more."

"It was pretty good, wasn't it?"

Annabelle nodded. There was nothing to be gained by complaining now.

Her father dumped the remainder of the fish into the old skillet Grandma used to collect table scraps for the dogs' supper. It was time to go back to Lincoln. Annabelle washed her hands and then said goodbye to the aunts. She and Karen climbed into the backseat of the car and sat waiting for her father to finish re-telling the story of the fish to Aunt Mary. Annabelle put her legs together with her heels touching, like a mermaid's tail, the way she had the last time she'd listened to her father read.

Together, they hadn't gotten to the part where the little mermaid drank the potion and then grew legs. Annabelle read that part alone. The handsome prince found her; but without her tongue, she couldn't tell him how she loved him. He married another girl, and the mermaid was swept away to become a spirit of the air, one of a group who roamed the world performing good works. The air spirits flew into people's houses. They smiled with joy at good children and cried tears of sorrow when they saw naughty or wicked ones. And that was the end of story, a conclusion which Annabelle had found deeply unsatisfying. It sounded like something her mother would have written in an attempt to make Annabelle behave. Annabelle could almost hear her mother saying, What if the little mermaid has flown into the house? You wouldn't want to make her weep, would you? Not after all she's suffered.

Annabelle decided she was through with fairy tales. Now she'd only read stories about the magical candy that allowed fat women to shrink or articles about creepy relatives who tried to touch girls in places they shouldn't: stories that could tell her things she didn't know.

Her father started the car and they moved slowly down the long driveway that led to the main road. In her stomach, the fish sloshed around in all the milk Annabelle had consumed to wash it down. She looked out the back window to watch Babe and Lady running behind them. Every Saturday they followed the car to the end of the driveway, Lady yapping and Babe, as always, silent. No one had ever heard her bark, and Annabelle wondered if the reason for Babe's silence was something she would eventually learn, something she could come to understand, along with the hairdresser's knowledge, the purpose of the pads, and the meaning of *lesbian*. She raised her hand to wave goodbye to the dogs. Was there a physical reason, like the mermaid's cut-out tongue, that prevented Babe from barking, or had it been a decision Babe had made—a choice—to go through life without uttering a sound?

The Usual Punishment

On the witness stand, his mother refused to say Charlie had anything wrong with his mind, even though the lawyer had told her, *If we don't prove he's insane, he's going to die.*

For his last supper, Charlie Starkweather chose cold cuts over steak. Behind bars, in his blue jeans and workshirt, he licked salt and grease from his fingers. When the lawmen arrived to take him to the execution chamber, Charlie asked, "What's your hurry?" First, they had to cut a block of fabric out of the leg of his pants to expose his knee, and then one knelt to shave the hair off Charlie's calf.

Fabric flapping around his shaven leg, wrists cuffed, he walked along the slick linoleum. Years ago, following him home from grade school, the other kids had made fun of his bow-legged walk. "Who shot your horse?" they liked to shout. Now, instead of recalling that old torment, he should have been thinking of what had brought him here: the love of his life, Caril Fugate, that love gone wrong, the way one killing made the ones that followed easier, how during those days of running he'd been conscious of his own competence, the same way he'd felt lifting heavy garbage cans to dump in the back of the truck. A mindless reliance on the body's functionality. You could take comfort in that.

The electric chair looked like an old piece of Mission Oak on someone's porch, though rigged up with wires and boxes as if an enterprising boy had got ahold of it and tried to make a spaceship.

"Sit," the warden said.

Shouldn't fear make him resist? But the chair seemed like the usual punishment he'd known growing up—tied to one of the captain's chairs in the dining room, his arms and legs bound by rope his father jerked tight, muttering, "*Told* you to stay out of the street." Or, "Take money out of your mother's purse and then *lying* about it. Jesus." One time he'd been working on an art project, surrounded by cut shapes of paper and the smell of pencil lead. He dug his fingers into the pot of grainy paste and paused. Was it really made from the bodies of old horses, like they said?

Charlie sniffed. It didn't smell like meat. He put a blob against his tongue. The taste wasn't bad: sticky, all right, but with a comforting blandness. Faintly salty. Charlie'd eaten half the little container when his father came in, caught him chewing, and went for the rope. The chair's frame pressed hard against Charlie's spine, his arms pinned at elbow and wrist, rope wound around his torso, legs tied at knee and ankle. "What the hell is wrong with you?" his father asked, grunting a little as he tightened the knots.

At first the punishment was punishment: Charlie felt trapped, suffocated by the rope, the way a boy must feel in a boa constrictor's embrace. But after a while, it didn't seem so bad— better, after all, than the strap. Charlie thought about Harry Houdini and considered how he might free himself from these constraints and stride into the living room, throw a punch at his father's startled face and laugh.

Maybe the chair was easier for his father than the beatings, too. Tied down, Charlie sat quietly, after the initial expected fuss, as if he'd thought things over and was deciding how to mend his ways, instead of deciding, as he did, on how he would get revenge, on all the ways he would make them sorry.

And here in the chamber is like the end of a gangster movie he watched from the back row of the Joyo Theater. A hooded man fits the strapped mask over Charlie's face and mouth. He can't see. Hands attach an electrode to his knee. Against Charlie's fingers, the chair's arm is smooth as ice. *Any last words?* He shakes his head. The leather bands around his arms and chest jerk tight. He waits to hear his father's voice— *"Teach* you a *lesson"*—and tastes again the grit and salt of paste.

Three Versions of the Truth

I f you are a native of Lincoln, Nebraska, you understand many things about the town a newcomer does not. You can explain, for instance, why the pastries sold in Ideal Grocery are called Miller and Paine cinnamon rolls; you can identify which fraternity Johnny Carson joined at the University of Nebraska; you know the reason teenagers spend spring evenings stumbling around the fields in the south part of town, looking for Robber's Cave.

A native of Lincoln understands how history connects to place, as with the old Crest station on Cornhusker Highway. Charlie Starkweather shot the attendant there in 1958; he was alone for that first murder, but his fourteen-year-old girlfriend, Caril Fugate, accompanied him on the subsequent killing spree. She spent much of her life in prison. A fourteen-year-old girl, on the cusp of womanhood, falling for the wrong boy; Ellen Suskind thinks about Caril Fugate every time she drives past the Crest station, how one bad decision in love can ruin a person's future.

But even someone who's spent her whole life here, as Ellen has, can't be sure about what happened in the old Morgan house twenty-two years ago, during the dark hours before sunrise on a May morning in 1975. Rumors and facts have stewed together over the decades, a potent combination of privilege and filicide, insanity and guilt. Now, twenty-two years after the tragedy, three versions of the truth have evolved to explain why a mother killed her only daughter.

As a matter of fact, Ellen hasn't spent her whole life in Lincoln. For two years after she graduated from college, she was married and lived in North Carolina. Now that she's in her fifties, she maintains only a few fragmentary images of those years: her husband, the father of her daughter Katie, sitting on the hood of his TR-3; the thick wooded areas that loomed up everywhere, converging and closing in on her at night; the occasional shock of a Confederate flag, its intersecting bars in the same configuration as bones crossed under a skull.

When Katie was a year old, Ellen moved back to Lincoln, where she could stand outside and see flat landscape stretching around her, benign, visible all the way to the horizon. She got her real estate license, a decision that turned out to be one of her better ones, especially following, as it did, on the heels of the bad plan of marriage.

The Morgan house is located on Lancaster Boulevard, a two-mile-long street that curves through the south part of the city. While Lancaster may not be the *nicest* block in Lincoln, it is, as Ellen tells her clients, a *desirable* address. Doctors, lawyers, and university professors live in the large, well-kept houses. Lancaster is a place where attention is paid: manicured lawns; holidays commemorated with yard decorations of pumpkins, or wreaths, or inflatable Easter bunnies; clean front windows allow a view of clean, carefully-arranged rooms. In fact, Ellen and Katie live on Lancaster, though on the poor end of the boulevard, in a small house that required a lot of TLC. That's why Ellen was able to afford it. Even the poor end of Lancaster costs more than most people have to spend.

The Morgan house is four blocks from Ellen's house. She walks past it on the nightly strolls she takes through the neighborhood.

Now, twenty-two years after the tragedy, the house looks the same as ever: two stories of gray clapboard, dark green shutters beside the windows, a sun porch on the second floor next to the room that Ellen has been told was the daughter's room, a tennis court out back. No one lives in the house; after the girl—Rhonda—was killed, the Lutheran Church next door bought the place to use as office space. When the front door is open, Ellen can see the living room, where the church has put up a warren of cubicles and suspended ugly fluorescent lights from the high ceiling.

There were five Morgans, Mr. and Mrs., and the three kids, two boys and a girl. The girl, Rhonda, was the middle child. The youngest was Christopher, who Katie dated for a while in high school. Ellen can't remember the name of the older boy—a commonplace name, she's thinking, as she walks up the path to the front door two days before Halloween. The church has decided to sell the Morgan house, and they've hired Ellen as the listing agent. A commonplace name, she repeats to herself. John? Michael?

Up close, Ellen sees that the paint on the shutters has faded. The front door is unlocked. Inside, the air smells of burned coffee and old books. "Hello?" Ellen calls. Scratches scar the oak floors in the living room. Clusters of thumbtacks pierce the wallpaper above the fireplace. A few of the cubicles have been dismantled, but others still stand in place, their surfaces littered with Post-it notes. The church will be using the house for another month, she's been told, but they wanted to go ahead and get it on the market. They know it's going to be hard to sell.

"Hello?" Ellen calls again. No one seems to be in the house, though Ellen has a sense—her overactive imagination, she tells herself, and that's something she's going to have to curb before she starts showing clients through—of a presence, benign enough, because she's not frightened, simply conscious of being not exactly alone as she measures the rooms on the main floor and makes notes on a legal pad. *Stunning back yard with tennis court. Needs some updating, but so much potential! Large fireplace in kitchen. Your good taste will transform this home into a showplace!*

For some reason, she can't bring herself to mount the steps to the second floor. She decides to measure the upstairs tomorrow, and leaves, gently closing the door behind her. She takes a For Sale sign out of the trunk of her car and wedges it into the ground, which is still soft. The weather's been unusually warm for October; it's hard to believe Halloween is only two days away. Up and down the block, pumpkins grin on porches. The neighbors next door to the Morgan house have decorated a tree with ornaments in the shape of ghosts. The little figures twist and sway in the breeze. Cute idea, Ellen thinks. The ghosts and pumpkins remind her that she needs to get Halloween candy.

Driving back to her office, Ellen tries to put out of her mind the ironic coincidence of the Morgan house going up for sale two days before Halloween.

The irony—would Katie appreciate it? She needs to call Katie, who's living in Oregon, and admit that she's listing the house. Otherwise she'll look like she's aware that the Morgans are an issue on which she and Katie are divided.

She will get candy tonight, Ellen tells herself. And she will call Katie tomorrow. Promise.

Katie was ten the spring Rhonda was killed, a Sunday in late May, the last week of school. It was the day Katie had called her father to tell him she no longer wanted to spend two weeks of her summer vacation in North Carolina. She didn't like the creepy woods, she had no friends there, somebody had called her a "damn Yankee" when she said she was from Nebraska. Ellen told Katie she understood, but Katie would have to explain her reasons to her father. The terse telephone call took place after lunch. Afterwards,

Katie said, "I feel bad, but I feel relieved, too," which Ellen found to be a healthily ambivalent reaction.

Since the afternoon was warm, they went outside. Ellen began spading up the flower bed next to the front porch. An ambulance howled past on Lancaster, and Ellen heard its siren stop abruptly, not far away. She glanced at her watch—it was a little past two-thirty in the afternoon—and, carrying the spade, walked to the sidewalk, where she peered down the street, though a slight curve in the road prevented her from seeing further than a block or two. Katie, sitting on the porch swing reading one of Ellen's old Nancy Drew mysteries, looked up from her book.

Lilacs bloomed along the island that divided the east and west bound lanes of traffic. Bees hung over the spirea bushes marking the property line between Ellen and her neighbor. After the siren stopped, the air rang with silence. Ellen had no idea that four blocks away, a girl had been discovered dead in her bedroom, and a woman—a mother—a few years older than Ellen herself, and divorced, like Ellen, was being gently questioned by the chief of police.

She looked at Katie and shrugged. Katie shrugged back, and Ellen returned to turning dirt in her garden.

She worked on the yard for a couple of hours. Katie finished the Nancy Drew mystery and went inside to do homework. The sun began its decent, casting a buttery glow over the neighborhood. Almost dinner time, Ellen thought. She was carrying the shovel toward the garage when she noticed a car creeping along Lancaster Boulevard. It stopped in front of her house. Ellen sensed the occupants regarding her. Perhaps they were lost, wanting to ask directions. She looked toward them, shading her eyes. The car's windows were down, and she heard one of the passengers say, "That must be her."

Odd, Ellen thought. She walked toward the car, carrying the shovel. She had no idea at the time—though she would understand, once she read the paper the following morning—that these people had heard about the Morgan murder over a police scanner and went looking for the house. Now they thought they'd found it, but they had the wrong address. The Morgan house was at 2818 Lancaster, and Ellen's address was 3218, four blocks away. But these gawkers, Ellen would realize later, believed that her house was the Morgan house, that she herself was Sallie Morgan, and as she approached the car to ask if they needed something, the passengers looked at her with horror, rolled up their windows, and the car sped away.

The reason for the passengers' reaction became clear to Ellen the following morning when she opened the Lincoln *Star*. Sallie Morgan, a "socialite," had been taken into custody after one of the Morgan boys, curious as to why his sister hadn't left her bedroom by two in the afternoon, went upstairs and found the girl's body. He called his father. The Morgans had been divorced for almost a year, and the father lived a couple of miles away with his new wife. After the phone call, Mr. Morgan went to the house on Lancaster. He phoned the chief of police. Ellen wondered who had called the ambulance, the father or one of the boys. Those poor boys, Ellen thought. She stirred a spoonful of sugar into her coffee and looked out the kitchen window for a minute before she continued reading.

Rhonda Morgan had been a student at Irving Junior High, the school Katie would attend in a few years. A small, grainy photo of Rhonda was centered in the column of print. She had long, light-colored hair and dark eyes. She'd been a bright student, the principal said. President of Student Council, president of the junior Red Cross. Ellen parsed these details: Rhonda had been both popular and conscientious. A good girl.

She was strangled with the cord of a woman's robe. The time of death, the coroner estimated, was six in the morning. One of the boys reported that his mother hadn't been home when he got up about nine a.m. She'd left a note that she'd gone to the early service at church, and that story was corroborated by several witnesses who'd sat near Sallie Morgan in the pews of St. Mark's. She seemed normal, one witness reported. The only strange thing was she'd walked, and the church was a long ways from her house, almost two miles. In high heels, too.

How long did Ellen sit there, the paper open before her, the swirl of details—the good girl, the strangling, the mother going to church afterwards—refusing to congeal into any coherent narrative? No wonder the car of strangers had stared at her yesterday, then driven away as if they'd seen the devil!

She heard Katie padding through the living room. Sun shone through the kitchen window; a breeze teased the hems of the curtains. It was a beautiful day.

"What's wrong?" Katie asked when she saw Ellen's face.

Ellen stood, dumped her cold coffee in the sink, and poured herself a fresh cup. "I need to tell you something," she said, and Katie carefully settled herself into the kitchen chair across from Ellen. She folded her hands on top of the table. She waited.

Ellen explained how terrible things sometimes happen, even in your own neighborhood; not four blocks away, a girl a little older than Katie had been killed, and suspicion centered around the girl's mother.

Katie's mouth hung open. Her long hair, a sandy blond she'd gotten from her father, stroked across the table when she leaned forward. "Why?"

"I don't know."

Katie stared at Ellen, blinking.

"It was an aberration," Ellen said.

"What's *aberration*?"

"A strange, awful thing." Ellen put her hand on Katie's hand. Katie's expression was the same one she'd worn the day Ellen had explained menstruation—a combination of disgust and puzzlement, as if Ellen were making up something purely to test

Katie's credulity: the blood, the unpredictability of its arrival, the preparations and precautions, the potential discomfort of cramps. As if your own body would betray you that way!

"Where is she?" Katie asked.

"Who?"

"The mother."

Ellen glanced down at the newspaper. "It says she was taken into custody. So that means she's in jail."

Katie nodded. "Will she get out?"

"I don't know."

Twenty-two years later, Ellen wonders if Katie remembers that morning. It's the day before Halloween. A bowl of miniature Snickers sits in the middle of the kitchen table. Ellen unwraps one and bites into the chocolate. How clear that conversation remains to her: the curtains blowing in the breeze, the old pink T-shirt Katie'd slept in, the way Katie pulled her knees up against her chest, under the T-shirt. With just her feet peeking out from the hem, she looked like a Thalidomide baby sitting at the table. Neither of them knew that morning that Katie would end up dating Christopher Morgan, the brother of the dead girl.

Ellen dials Katie's number in Oregon and waits while the phone rings and rings. No answer. Maybe Katie and her husband are still asleep. Maybe they've gone out to breakfast; maybe they're having an argument that can't be interrupted. Katie is always telling Ellen how much she and Mark argue, though she presents it in a comical way, as if their lives are filled with the sort of slapstick disagreements you see between Lucy and Ricky Ricardo. Ellen likes Mark, but it's hard for her to formulate a clear opinion of Katie's marriage. When the answering machine clicks on, Ellen leaves a message for Katie to call her. "Nothing important. Whenever you get time," she says. "I have some funny news."

Ellen drives the four blocks to the Morgan house. Pulling into the driveway, she sees her friend Pat Stephenson exiting the side door. She carries a coffee maker. Ellen steps out of the car and waves. Pat is the Director of Religious Education at the Lutheran Church, and she recommended Ellen to be the listing agent. On the one hand, Ellen is grateful; the house is large and on a desirable street, so a sale holds the potential for a large commission. On the other hand, the possibility exists that the place will stay on the market for months and months, that the only people Ellen will show through will be locals—gawkers—who haven't forgotten after twenty-two years and want to see for themselves the room where the murder took place.

"I'll be back in about an hour," Pat calls. "I have to find some space at the church for all this stuff—"

"That's fine," Ellen calls back. She sees a man standing by the first floor sun porch, his back to her, peering through the window. He wears a red windbreaker, which suggests to Ellen that he's a local; red and white are the colors of the beloved Cornhusker football team, and people in Lincoln favor red clothing as an expression of loyalty. The first gawker, Ellen thinks, walking toward him. She suppresses a sigh.

"Hello," Ellen says. When the man turns, she's so startled that she feels her hand moving involuntarily to cover her mouth. It's Christopher Morgan. Christopher Morgan! She had no idea he was still in Lincoln. She hasn't seen him in what—ten years? Twelve? She imagines the bright, professional smile she'd assumed now looks brittle and forced, the raised hand a visible sign of shock. She covers her mouth and coughs. "Christopher," she says, at the same moment he says, "Mrs. Suskind! How are you?"

"I'm fine," Ellen says. "And you? I didn't know you were still in town."

"I'm only here for a visit," he says. "I live in Maine now."

"Maine!" Ellen says. One of the big trees on the edge of the property creaks in the wind. A few leaves skate across the lawn. "That's a long ways away."

He shrugs. His face looks almost the same, but Ellen notices his skin—like the house's shutters—seems a little faded, and lines around his eyes make him appear tired.

"I always come back in the fall to go to a football game with my father, and he told me he'd driven by here yesterday and saw the house was for sale—"

Ellen nods, still smiling. She is consumed with the feeling she'd always experienced around Christopher: an anxiety about saying the wrong thing. Should she acknowledge he'd had a sister? If she asked about his father, did she also need to ask about his mother? If she asked about his mother, would she sound friendly and concerned or pruriently interested?

"I wondered if it still looks the same inside," Christopher says.

He wants to see the house, Ellen realizes. "I need to measure the upstairs rooms, if you'd like to come in," she says. "It's kind of a mess—the church is still moving things out—"

"I don't mind." Christopher tucks his hands in the pockets of his jacket. "It's funny, you know, when I saw your name on the for sale sign and your home phone number, it was still so familiar to me." He recites the number.

"Well," Ellen says. "You've certainly got a good memory." Christopher shrugs again, and they walk toward the front door.

On Tuesday, the second day after the Morgan murder, the *Star* ran a picture of Mrs. Morgan and her attorney walking to the courtroom for her arraignment. Sallie Morgan wore a light-colored, sleeveless top and a dark skirt. Her shoulder-length hair looked a little disheveled and her head dipped down, her gaze on the ground, the posture people in Lincoln adopt on icy sidewalks when they need to keep an eye on the footing ahead. The lawyer walked half a pace ahead of her, holding her elbow, his arm connecting the two of them like a leash stretched between a recalcitrant dog and its hurried owner.

The accompanying article relied heavily on an anonymous

sheriff's deputy, who explained what he'd seen in the police report. In the early morning of May 27th, Sallie Morgan had gone to her daughter's room. Light flickered under the door, and when she stepped inside, she saw the whole room was ablaze, and Rhonda, in bed, was on fire. On fire! Ellen thought. The skin of her arms constricted with horror.

Sallie Morgan had put a pillow over Rhonda's face in an attempt to smother the flames. She didn't mean to kill the girl; she was trying to save her from burning alive. The deputy thought she must have been hallucinating, in the grip of mental illness.

Christ, Ellen thought. Still, a certain coherence existed in this version of events. The craziness supplied a motive. Only a crazy woman would kill her child; daughters with normal mothers had nothing to worry about. The article had made Ellen's hands sweat against the newspaper, and she looked at her fingers, darkened as if with soot.

Ellen holds open the front door and motions for Christopher to go inside. She wonders what it's like, returning to a place you'd once lived, probably once been happy, a place now tainted by the tragedy that forced you out. "Wow," Christopher says as he walks into the living room. "It's just the same."

And surely it is; redecorating would have been a frivolous expenditure for the church, so they left the wallpaper Sallie Morgan had chosen on the walls, the curtains she'd selected hanging over the windows. Ellen sees Christopher wince when he looks down at the oak floor in the living room. "My mother always made us take off our shoes," he said. "She was afraid we'd scratch the floor." He steps close to the fireplace, then kneels and points at a cluster of round indentations in the wood, each one about the circumference of a thumbtack. "Mrs. Satterfield did that. She was wearing those really thin high heels—what do you call them?"

"Stilettos," Ellen says. Looking down at Christopher, she sees a quarter-sized bald spot on the crown of his head.

"Yes. And she was sort of a heavy woman, you know, and her weight on the heels made those marks on the floor. Boy," Christopher says, "my mother was mad."

Ellen smiles. On the one hand, it's a funny story—the weight of a heavy woman hammering her own shoes into the floor—but at the same time she feels a little chill at the detail of Christopher's mother's anger. Anger, after all, was the emotion behind another version of the Morgan tragedy, the revenge story.

According to the revenge story, Sallie Morgan had discovered her husband was having an affair. She filed for divorce on the grounds of extreme mental cruelty. (This, Ellen knew, was true. She'd seen the divorce listed in the *Star's* Daily Record column. But why mental cruelty, why not adultery? To Ellen, they sounded equally bad.) The divorce was granted; Mrs. Morgan received custody of the three children and a generous alimony settlement, as well as the house. Mr. Morgan married the other woman. (All this was true, too.)

But even with the children, the alimony, the nice house on Lancaster Boulevard, Sallie Morgan was consumed with rage. Her husband had left her for a younger woman; he'd lied when he'd said his wedding vows. She would show him, the story went. She would show him what happened when you wronged a woman who'd sacrificed her life for you.

Ellen had wondered if some Greek tragedy had inspired this version of the Morgan story when she first heard it from Pat Stephenson. The idea that Sallie Morgan planned to kill *all* the children in some complicated pattern—the girl first, strangled, then the older boy, who was going to be shot; Pat wasn't quite sure about the plan for Christopher—struck Ellen as farfetched beyond credibility. No one would do that, not even a crazy person.

Still, the factual parts of the story coated the rest with a veneer of truth, and this version continued circulating for years. Ellen has always wondered if the Morgan boys knew of it, if they'd overheard some stranger talking about how close they'd come to death.

Ellen turns and leads the way to the sunroom. "So what took you to Maine?" she asks Christopher.

In the sunroom, bookshelves line the walls, filled with Bibles and hymnals. Christopher touches the spine of one of the Bibles. He isn't wearing a wedding ring. "I'm an architect. Residential."

"Now did you go to school in Maine?" Ellen knows he didn't go to school there, but he hasn't exactly answered her question: why Maine? Surely an architect could find a job anywhere.

"No, I went to Brown, then graduate school at the University of Michigan."

"That's right," Ellen says. She only knew about Brown; he and Katie lost touch during college.

"I moved to Maine because my wife—my ex-wife—that was her home state."

"It's supposed to be beautiful there, isn't it?"

"It's cold," Christopher says. "Woodsy. I'm thinking about moving."

"Kids?" Ellen asks.

"No." He brushes his hand against his leg. "Maybe I could move back to Lincoln. Maybe I could buy this house."

The sunroom's walls are papered with a dark paisley pattern; outside, a layer of clouds have obscured the sun, so the room is dim, making it easier for Ellen to look Christopher right in the eye. "Well, it's for sale," she says, hoping her tone hits the right light note.

"How much?"

Ellen tells him.

"Not bad," Christopher says. "I always forget how cheap things are in Lincoln."

Is he serious? Ellen wonders. Why would he want to move back into this house?

"You know how it is," Christopher continues. "After getting divorced, wanting to come back home."

Katie must have told him, years ago, that was exactly what Ellen had done. "I understand," she says.

"So how is Katie doing?"

"Katie's doing fine. She and her husband live in Oregon."

"Oregon," Christopher says. "I've never been there."

Someone bangs around in the kitchen, probably packing up the extra kitchen supplies the church used for soup suppers and wedding receptions. The sunroom smells of the old bindings of the Bibles. Ellen can't help thinking, guiltily: Katie not exactly happy, Christopher divorced—maybe they should have stayed together, two negatives joining to make a positive.

But of course, who knew? Who could make a prediction whether a high school romance would evolve into a long, happy marriage? How could anyone see into the future?

The middle of July, six weeks after the Morgan murder, Ellen sat on the cement around Eden Pool with a group of mothers. Grass outside the fence had turned brown from the heat. The sky was the same blue as the pool's water. Ellen noticed the different colors around them—the grass, the sky, the gray cement, darker in spots where wet footprints led to the snack bar—while the other mothers talked about the possibility of the Morgan kids showing up here to swim. Eden Pool was in the area of the Morgan's neighborhood; perhaps not the public pool closest to their house—that would be Irving Pool, next to the junior high—but a conceivable destination for the Morgan kids. The remaining Morgan kids. If the remaining Morgan kids still lived in the house on Lancaster Boulevard. Did Ellen know?

By July, Ellen was tired of listening to people talk about the murder. She shaded her eyes to see Katie poised on the low diving board. She wanted to call, "Be careful!" but she knew that would only embarrass her daughter. And the issue of which public pool the Morgan kids might swim in was a moot point. The Morgans belonged to the Country Club, so of course they would go swimming there.

"Ellen?" Pat Stephenson said. "Is anybody still living in the Morgan house?"

"I don't think so," Ellen said. "There never seem to be any lights on at night, and no cars in the driveway."

"They'll never be able to sell it," Pat said. "After what happened there."

Ellen heard a splash, and she looked at the blue water, right at the spot where Katie raised her head, smiling.

As Pat predicted, the Morgan house sat on the market for months. The law of latent defects required disclosure of the murder to prospective buyers, and so anyone who didn't know about the Morgan tragedy before they went in the house had to be told before they made an offer to purchase. Finally, the summer following the murder, the Lutheran Church next door bought the house to use as office space. The sale served as a reasonable accommodation, a sort of exorcism, linking the place of tragedy with a house of God. No one would actually be living there, waking at night and wondering if the noise he'd heard were the boards settling or ghostly footsteps, tree branches scraping against windows, or a girl's voice saying *No! Stop!*

Katie met Christopher Morgan at Irving Junior High. They had a lot of classes together: American Literature, typing, Spanish. At first, when Katie talked about Christopher, her voice held a tone of awe. He seemed so normal, considering he'd gone through that terrible tragedy everyone knew about. But after awhile, her awe disappeared. He became just another boy with a past of no consequence.

In high school, Katie and Christopher both joined the drama club. They belonged to a small pack of students who did things together on the weekends—eight or ten of them went to the high school football games in the fall, the basketball games in the winter and spring, out for pizza at Godfather's or Valentino's.

Ellen liked Katie's friends, who were bright and pleasant, occasionally unconventional. Julie, Katie's best friend, for instance, liked to wear clothes she found at the Goodwill—old bowling shirts with a man's name stitched on the chest, or jewel-necked cardigans embroidered with sequins. In the fall of their senior year, Katie and Julie spent hours talking about where they wanted to go for college. Out west, to California, where it was always sunny and you could run into movie stars on the streets. Or to the East Coast, some storied school like Yale where the buildings had existed longer than Nebraska had even been a state.

Ellen told Katie places like that were expensive, that she'd have to keep her grades up and get a good scholarship offer, and then they'd see.

Ellen knew she was fortunate Katie was having such an easy adolescence. Of course Katie occasionally became moody, giving Ellen a stone-faced look when Ellen suggested she should be doing homework instead of watching television or talking on the phone. Sometimes Katie burst into tears when she felt overwhelmed by one of her AP assignments. Still, it was nothing like the stories Ellen heard from Pat Stephenson, whose daughter Anna was a year older than Katie: staying out all night, clothes reeking of cigarettes—at least Pat hoped it was cigarettes and not something else—and the sullen boyfriend who stood mute as a criminal when Pat asked about his plans for college. Pat hoped Anna was just going through a phase. "Sometimes I'd like to strangle her," Pat said, and even though years had passed since the Morgan murder, she added quickly, "I'm kidding."

"I know," Ellen said. "Of course you're kidding."

Christopher leads the way to the kitchen. An elderly woman—the person Ellen heard from the sunroom—smiles at them and then carries a box out the back door. Ellen is conscious that she and Christopher have reversed roles. Instead of Ellen doing the talking—pointing out how a coat of white paint could really brighten things up, that the floors could be refinished to sand out the scratches—Christopher tells Ellen about the house. "This was the thing I loved best," he says about the big fireplace in the kitchen. His father built fires on winter Sundays, and his mother made omelets and heated up cinnamon rolls from Miller and Paine, the local department store, for breakfast. "I guess Miller and Paine went out of business?" Christopher says.

"Yes," Ellen tells him. "Back in 1988. But there's a bakery that still makes the cinnamon rolls. You can get them at Ideal."

Christopher nods. They stand staring at the fireplace, which looks like one you'd find in a Colonial household, big enough to heat a whole room. Up close, Ellen smells burned wood.

Christopher says he remembers the day the tennis court in the back yard had been put in. He was only three at the time—the baby of the family—and his older brother, Dan, who was ten, was forced to help spade up the ground. "Dan says there's no way I can remember, that I was too young, but I think people do remember things from a very early age. Katie told me she remembered when you moved into the house on Lancaster. How old was she then?"

"Two," Ellen says. They're walking back through the living room, toward the master suite. "What did she remember?"

"She said you took her into the room that was going to be hers and said, 'This is your bedroom. You can do anything you want in here.'"

Ellen laughs. "*I* don't even remember that."

"Katie had a very good memory," Christopher says. They're standing on the threshold of the master suite. He looks at Ellen and Ellen has to look away.

A rough-textured, taupe-colored paper covers the walls. The curtains are black and taupe. Christopher says his mother redecorated the room after his father left. His sister helped pick out the wallpaper. Christopher didn't like it with everything so dark and gloomy. He remembers the room better the way it had been before, with pale green walls and white curtains, even though the room had been pretty much off limits to the kids; he only went in if one of his parents wanted to have a private conversation with him. It was the place his mother sat when she needed peace and quiet.

Ellen says, "I imagine it would get—lively—with three kids."

"Yes," Christopher says. "It did sometimes."

Near the end of the summer of 1975, a final article about the Morgan murder appeared in the newspaper. A team of expensive psychiatrists had met with Sallie Morgan, and they determined that she had been mentally incompetent at the time her daughter was killed. She'd been "gripped by an intense involvement in religious fanaticism." She had hallucinated that the girl was on fire, and she had no idea, at the time of the killing, of what she was actually doing.

In light of these findings, the county attorney dropped the murder charge. Ellen saw him on television, at a press conference where he explained his decision. A crime is composed of two parts, the act itself and the mental state accompanying the act. Because Sallie Morgan was unable to formulate the required intent—she didn't mean to kill her daughter—she wasn't guilty of murder. She was released to the custody of her family, who sent her to a well-known clinic in Kansas, Meninger's, for treatment.

That, of course, should have been the end of the Morgan

incident. But people in Lincoln couldn't let it go. The case didn't seem *closed*. Questions hadn't been answered. For instance, which of the brothers had found Rhonda's body? Why was the girl killed, why not one of the boys? Why wasn't Sallie Morgan sent to the Lincoln Regional Center, which was what generally happened to the mentally incompetent? At least, to the mentally competent who didn't have... connections.

Some of the speculative answers were passed along as fact, and soon after Sallie Morgan had left for Kansas, a new angle on the Morgan murder evolved. Ellen wasn't sure where she first heard the version based on Sallie Morgan's depression; the story simply infiltrated the air, like the lingering smell of poison from insecticide that city trucks sprayed around Lincoln at the end of the summer.

In many ways, this story presented Sallie Morgan in the most sympathetic light. Ellen considered the details one night when she'd gone for a walk down Lancaster Boulevard and stopped in front of the vacant Morgan house. The depression story required you to take on Sallie Morgan's point of view, to try and understand how her life had fallen apart, to imagine this:

You are a girl growing up in the Midwest in the 1940's and '50's, you have a lovely face, some artistic talent, an ambition to marry well. Dreams you've discussed with your girlfriends, who have similar aspirations—but perhaps not as strong as *your* desire. And it seems, for a while, that everything you've wished for comes true: the successful husband, the agreeable children, the nice house on one of the nicest streets in town.

Then, what you never expected to happen happens. Another woman intrudes, the fabric of family life rips, shreds, burns; there's a divorce, and you're left on your own at age 39, forced by no desire of your own to start over. To start over! With what, for what? Certainly women exist who find inner strength in the wake of marital disaster. They make new, happy lives for themselves, single. But for you, it's different. The divorce cuts you adrift.

Your dreams are filled with drownings. Your perception of the world alters. Sunlight shining above the window seat lacks warmth; dust bunnies gather and multiply in the corners of rooms, fingerprints spot the walls around the light switches. Some days, you can't bring yourself to get out of bed. The universe has become a treacherous place, a place filled with heartbreak and disappointment particularly directed at *women*, ugliness and grief you believe your daughter must be protected from. She must not suffer the way you have suffered.

For someone in a crippling state of depression, the worst plans make a kind of sense. You have your reasons as you walk up the stairs to the second floor. Behind closed doors, your children breathe. Your hands grip the tie of your bathrobe. In endless sleep, you think, there will be peace.

For their first date, Katie and Christopher went to dinner at the Hunan Palace on O Street. A Friday in January, Ellen remembers. Cold. Katie stood in her bedroom, peering at herself in the dressing-table mirror. She had on a red sweater and lipstick. It was the first time Ellen had seen her wearing lipstick; it seemed a little old for her, but Ellen didn't say anything. After all, Katie was seventeen. When Ellen was in high school, everyone wore lipstick.

"Who all is going?" Ellen sat on her bed, untangling a gold chain Katie had found at the bottom of her jewelry box. Katie curled her hair with hot rollers and the room smelled of hot, freshly-shampooed hair.

"Just me and Christopher," she said. Ellen met her eyes in the mirror and she smiled with those bright, unfamiliar lips.

"So this is a date, then." Ellen went back to prying at the chain with her fingernails.

"I guess," Katie said. She was still smiling into the mirror. "I guess it is."

❦

After that first date, Katie and Christopher became a couple. They sloughed off the rest of the pack and spent all their time together: Christopher drove Katie to school in the mornings and home in the afternoons; they did homework in Katie's bedroom at night; on weekends, they went to movies or dinner. Sometimes they wandered around the fields south of town, looking for Robber's Cave, which was rumored to have been the hideout of Jesse James after an 1876 bank robbery. Supposedly he'd left money hidden in the cave's secret crevices.

After a couple of weeks, Ellen asked Katie, casually, whether Christopher ever talked about his mother. They stood in the kitchen, washing dishes after supper. "I always wondered what happened to her, where she ended up," Ellen said.

Katie went still. She held a plate between her hands. "Christopher doesn't like to talk about what happened," she said. Ellen heard—or thought she heard—a note of censure in her voice. As if Katie thought Ellen was *prying*.

"Oh," Ellen said. "Well, put the plate away if you're done drying it."

Katie's plans about college changed. She no longer cared about UCLA or Yale; instead, she and Christopher wanted to go to Brown together. "Try some other places, too," Ellen said, and Katie grudgingly sent an application to Nebraska.

In the spring of Katie's senior year, a letter from Brown University arrived. A thick letter. Ellen knew what it meant.

Katie shrieked with glee when she opened the envelope. She ran to the phone and called Christopher. Ellen kept herself secluded in the kitchen, deliberately *not listening* to their conversation, though she could hear occasional fragments: *We can go to football games! New York's how far?*

Ellen made a meatloaf. She baked chocolate chip cookies; she rolled a tray full of the cresent rolls Katie loved. At dinner, she let

Katie talk for a while about all the plans she had, and then she said, "Honey, how much is tuition?"

Katie cleared her throat and told Ellen the amount.

Ellen knew at the time—and she knows now, years later, following Christopher Morgan out of the master suite and heading toward the stairs that lead to the upper floor—that there were ways they could have afforded to send Katie to Brown. Loans, money from Katie's father, money Ellen herself had saved. Still, at the time, the amount was large enough to make her sit back in her chair. In Lincoln, you could buy a house for the cost of two years' tuition. One year's tuition would finance a whole undergraduate degree at the University of Nebraska and a couple of years in medical school. Ellen said, "That's a lot of money."

"But you've been saving, right?" Katie's chin trembled. "You've been saving, and I can get a job, and they said they'd give me a scholarship—"

"How much?"

"Two thousand."

"A semester?"

Katie lowered her eyes. "For the first year."

"I don't know how we can afford it," Ellen said. "I'm sorry, honey."

Katie cried and cried. Her eyes swelled. Her nose turned red. The following morning, even after applications of ice and slices of cucumber, she looked awful. She begged Ellen to call the high school and tell them she was sick. She'd go back to school the next day, she promised. But today, she had to stay home.

Ellen called the school. It was the least she could do.

Katie and Christopher continued dating, though Ellen sensed the issue of college had created a gap between them. She could overhear them talking—arguing—in Katie's bedroom. "Why can't you stay here?" Katie asked.

"I can't stay here," Christopher said. "Why can't you ask your father for the money?"

"We are *estranged*," Katie said, coldly.

They saw each other during the summer; in fact, Christopher helped Katie move boxes down to her dorm room in Cather Hall before he left for the east coast. But then a few weeks after Katie started her freshman year, she met a boy in the Phi Gamma Delta house. "That was the fraternity Johnny Carson belonged to," Ellen told her. "The Fijis." After the first Fiji, Katie dated a different Fiji for a semester, then a football player, and eventually Katie and Christopher lost track of each other completely. Just a high school romance, Ellen thinks as she follows Christopher up the stairs. At least, that's what Ellen has repeated to herself for years, *just a high school romance.*

At the top of the steps, Ellen takes a breath. After the spacious, high-ceilinged rooms on the main floor, she is surprised at how cramped the upper story seems. The stairs open onto a narrow hallway; Christopher turns left and goes into a playroom decorated in bright primary colors. Built-in shelves line the walls. Red beams span the ceiling. "This is nice," Ellen says. She takes a tape measure out of her purse and unspools it along the floor.

"It was never this clean when we lived here," Christopher says. He kneels and puts his index finger against the tape measure's tab to hold it in place. "We used to leave games out for weeks, and puzzles. My mother made us keep the door shut if company came."

Ellen wonders where Sallie Morgan has ended up. No one seems to know; Pat said she'd heard California, but Ellen was sure someone had told her the east coast.

Next to the playroom is the bathroom. *Full bath on second floor*, Ellen writes on her legal pad. Two doors on the north side of the hallway open onto bedrooms. "This was my room," Christopher says. A battered filing cabinet stands against one wall, with faded drawings taped above it. The windows look out on the

back lawn, the tennis court. Again, Christopher holds the tape
measure for Ellen. He's quiet now. She understands.

The other bedroom belonged to his brother. Ellen writes the
room's dimensions on her legal pad. The upper sun porch opens
off the brother's room. Christopher looks toward it, shrugs, and
then only the last bedroom remains, Rhonda's old room.

The door is shut. That night in May, did Sallie Morgan pause
here in the hallway, in the spot where Ellen stands, leaning toward
the door, listening to her daughter breathing inside? Now there's
a nameplate on the door: *Dr. Otis Robinson, Pastor.* Ellen raises
her hand to knock. The gesture must make her shift her weight,
because the floor creaks under her feet.

Years ago, she'd struck this same pose, standing outside Katie's
bedroom door, which hung open a bare inch, listening to Katie
and Christopher inside. It was winter, two or three weeks after
they'd started dating. They were talking about an accident
involving one of their classmates that had occurred the previous
summer at Branched Oak Lake. The girl had been waterskiing,
and the driver of the boat swerved too close to the shore. The girl
arced across the water and slammed into the dock. Christopher
had been there when it happened. His description was clear and
unembellished. Precise, Ellen thought at the time, oddly
compelling. He had a way with words, and that's why she stood
listening; she wanted to hear how the story ended.

Katie made little moaning noises in response to certain things
he said. "She couldn't walk, so Johnny carried her to the car."
They must have been sitting or lying on the bed; Ellen could hear
the springs squeak when one of them shifted around.

"Was she bleeding?" Katie asked.

"Yes." He told the number of stitches the girl had gotten at the
hospital—over fifty—and after a pause, Katie said, "There?"

"There," he said.

Katie moaned. "I can't even think about it," she said. Ellen
was embarrassed for her: the melodrama in her voice, as if she'd

forgotten that tragedy was something that could happen to anyone. How could she forget, with Christopher right there next to her? "Then don't," he said, softly. Ellen held her breath, listening for what would happen next. They might have kissed; there was a short silence, and then he said, "Katie?"

"Oh, Christopher," Katie said. The bedsprings squeaked. Ellen lowered her arm. The back of her throat felt swollen, as if she were on the verge of sneezing. The springs squeaked again. She thought she heard a zipper unzip. Were they—? Ellen felt a chill ripple across her back. After that story about the cheerleader's accident—all those stitches *there*—they were having sex?

It was a juxtaposition that she couldn't make sense of, like that part of the Morgan murder she'd never understood, the fire and the strangling. Ellen could accept Sallie Morgan—in the grip of psychosis—walking up the stairs, opening the door, seeing the fire, going into Rhonda's room. Ellen could accept the hallucination. But if you saw your daughter was on fire, wouldn't you use a pillow to smother the flames? And conceivably a woman in the midst of a psychotic episode, thinking she was smothering flames, could end up suffocating the girl with a pillow. But what Ellen couldn't make sense of was the fact that the girl was strangled with the belt of her mother's bathrobe. In Ellen's mind, seeing fire was one thing. Choking someone with a belt to put out that fire was something else.

"Oh," Katie said. "Christopher."

Christopher. Was his mother truly insane? If she was, Christopher might have inherited a propensity for madness himself. But what if Sallie Morgan wasn't crazy, but something worse: a woman who'd deliberately killed her daughter and then managed to hoodwink the psychiatrists? Hoodwink, or bribe. What would happen to Katie if she stayed with Christopher and things went wrong?

Ellen crept away from the bedroom door. Months later, she acted in Katie's best interests when she said that they couldn't afford to send her to Brown. The cost of tuition had seemed like a gift, a sign from the universe that Katie and Christopher weren't meant to be together. For years, Ellen was able to tell herself that she hadn't really interfered with their relationship; they might have broken up anyway, even if they'd gone to college together; and if Christopher *really* loved Katie, he could have gone to school in Lincoln, too. In Lincoln, where Ellen could keep an eye on things.

But of course Christopher couldn't stay. He couldn't stay in this town where people never forgot. He needed to move to a place where no one knew he was the son of woman who had killed her daughter, where no one had an opinion about what had happened in his life, where there weren't people like Ellen who passed judgment on him because of something over which he'd had no control.

Ellen takes a deep breath. Christ, she'd been wrong. And now, what is the best way to make amends: by silence, or by acknowledgment and apology? The coward in Ellen whispers, *Least said, soonest mended.* Her knuckles bump against the bedroom door, an involuntary flinch, not a real knock.

She will say she's sorry that things didn't work out between him and Katie. That she'd always liked him; that Katie doesn't seem one hundred percent happy, that maybe Christopher and Katie would have been better off together. She should have figured out a way to send Katie to Brown. She will tell him this when they go inside the room.

Ellen flexes her wrist to knock again.

And then Christopher puts his hand over Ellen's hand. His fingers are cool and dry, his hand the size of a man's hand. It's odd for Ellen to think of him as an adult since he'd remained fixed in her mind all these years as a boy. Frozen in time, like a fossil lodged in rock, waiting to be discovered. He pulls her arm down, gently, and tucks it against her side. "That's okay," he says. "I didn't want to go in that room, anyway."

Aeneas Leaves Kansas

I will tell you, then, of my husband, a man who loved guns, who spent hours stroking an old petticoat along the barrel of his shotgun until it gleamed coldly, like the moon in December. Even then he might have been imagining the petticoat's ruffles were the foam of waves curving their way into shore.

Some saw in his silence a man of singular virtue, strong will. I saw in his silence an absence. A longing in him that the great fields of wheat dying in the drought tindered, as did the sound of the locusts that descended in punishment for what sin I don't know. That morning in August, I first thought the dark cloud moving toward us brought rain, but instead insects fell from the sky. We gathered the boys; we boarded the windows and closed ourselves in the house. Still, all night their grinding jaws chewed through the darkness.

I heard that people went mad from the sound. I heard that some fool of a woman went out to the dead wheat to drive them away. Those locusts devoured the clothes off her body and left her to stumble naked back to the house, her body streaked brown with their spit.

Two days later, we woke to silence. The wheat had been eaten down to the ground. The sun blazed on a land that was nothing but dirt. The harvest is past, the summer is ended, and we are not saved. My husband packed his guns in the buggy, hitched up the mare, and said he'd send for us when he could. He didn't say where he was headed.

In town, the talk went that he'd been lured away by some woman, a *goddess*. I turned a deaf ear; I had my own explanation. How often had he talked in his sleep, repeating the word *shore* over and over. I figured he'd gone east or west, drawn by the water.

The boys have stayed here, tied to the plow. I waited and wait. The seasons shift; the horses grow gray around their muzzles. Every spring arrives greener than the one before, and in those balmy days I think: Surely he'll return. From the front porch of our house, I look over the furrowed fields, those raised rows of earth. See that, I'd tell him if he were here. Don't they look like waves?

Why We Are the Way We Are

D ANGER

We were told that the city of Lincoln lay in the precise center of the United States. On maps, the Russians marked our hometown as the place they'd drop the atom bomb when they decided to wipe out the capitalist pigs forever. We'd be annihilated like Japanese civilians had been during World War II, the first Americans to die under clouds of radiation, the poisonous fires.

A grisly fact but one we savored, because did it not also reveal our distinction, our significant place in the world?

FIELDS

My father's family farm was located some miles beyond the city limits. In the summer, my father and the uncles went out to burn marijuana plants that grew wild in the ditches. With handkerchiefs tied around the lower parts of their faces, they looked like bandits. They took their cigarette lighters and boxes of matches; Grandpa hitched one of the horses to a wagon to haul pails of water in case the fire got out of control.

I was told to stay in the house. From the porch, I watched the men heading toward the ditch. Billows of smoke rose against the sky. There was yelling, to get back, to get some water. The fire cackled as it consumed the weeds. An intriguing odor filled the air—not the same as burned leaves, but a smell like gasoline that I wanted to sniff and sniff at the same time it made me a little sick and light-headed.

BEST FRIENDS

The first time I talked to you, I told the story about the ditchweed. We'd gotten assigned the same table in Mrs. Murphy's sophomore contemporary lit class, and she said, Introduce yourselves by telling something that distinguishes you from your classmates.

When I mentioned ditchweed, its compelling, gasoline-like odor, the two other people at the table—pimply boys—were shocked, but you laughed and said you, too, liked the way gasoline smelled.

We had lunch together that day, and every day after that. What an easy friendship to fall into! We thought the same things were funny. We wore the same styles of clothes. How lucky we were to have met, we told each other. As the months passed, it seemed like any situation that one of us experienced alone didn't really happen until the two of us talked it over. We told each other the most minute details of our lives: fights with our mothers, what we'd eaten for lunch, what we wished we'd eaten instead. How bad our cramps were, what boys said to us on the phone, what we said back, what we'd really been thinking at the time.

In our respective homes, we tied up the phones for hours to analyze ourselves, to discuss *why we are the way we are.* You dragged the phone in the bathroom, locked the door, and turned on the fan so no one in your family could hear what you said.

PLACES AND PEOPLE

There was always some place to go: Henry Park, where we sat under the big elm tree in my MG and drank Tanqueray mixed with Hawaiian Punch. Miller and Paine—Nebraska's Quality Department Store—where we both worked, you in the Book and

Camera department on the main floor, and me upstairs in China, where I copied down the choices brides made for their wedding registries. The Bistro (our favorite place for lunch), El Ranchito, where they didn't card, your house, my house, a party at 24th and J Street. School.

The boys we dated in high school were connected to places in the city. Their great-grandfathers had been the first people to ride into Lincoln on the main street—a dirt road, back then— look around, and decide to fulfill a need of the growing town. The need for food, or livery, or clothing. Their last names were scrolled across the storefronts and across paper sacks we carried around with our purchases inside: sneakers from K—'s, dresses from H—'s, birth control pills from W— Drug.

FIELDS

Fields surrounded Lincoln outside the city limits. Abandoned fields, we believed, when we were in high school. Every weekend in the fall, somebody would load a keg in the back of a car and drive out into the middle of one of the fields and we'd have a party. Night, November, the beer icy cold in plastic cups, a half-moon overhead, too many stars to count, a vast silence stretching beyond the little knot of noise we made, our feet flattening weeds against the frozen ground, our breath puffing in front of our faces when we talked, the way wolves' breath must puff when they howl in the cold.

DANGER

A couple years before either of us were born, a garbage man named Charlie Starkweather began dating a fourteen-year-old girl, Caril Fugate. Charlie was, by all accounts, destined for mediocrity or worse, and worse came to pass when one winter afternoon he murdered Caril's family, then took her—hostage, she claimed; willingly, others said—on a rampage of killing that the citizens of Lincoln would never forget.

Law enforcement officers captured Charlie and Caril in western Nebraska. He was tried, found guilty, and executed in the electric chair. After a long prison term, Caril was eventually released and moved to Michigan. She always claimed she was innocent. But we longed to know her whole story, what it must have been like to find yourself with someone who felt he had to prove his love the way that Charlie did.

BEST FRIENDS

Winter. Snow in the fields; packed snow on the roads. You and H— in the backseat of the Oldsmobile, me and B— in the front. Parked along the ditch outside of town, late night, engine running so there'd be heat and music. Tom Petty on the radio: Breakdown, he sang, Go ahead and give it to me—.

Those big old cars, with seats long enough to lie down on. I heard the springs squeak in the back seat; you moaned.

That moment was likely the precise one when your trouble started.

WHAT OUR MOTHERS SAID

Diet. Buck up. Famous last words. Don't count your chickens before they hatch. Make do.

BEST FRIENDS

You called, took the phone into the bathroom, turned on the fan, and cried. I knew immediately what was wrong—after all, the main topic of conversation for the past two weeks had been the fact you were late. Late, still late, still late.

All right, I said. Tell me what you want to do.

FIELDS

Afterwards, we drove out to Saltillo Road. It was late April, late in the afternoon. The sun burned brightly as it set. Green shoots were coming up in the fields. We sat in my car, close to the spot where your trouble started, and smoked cigarettes until you felt composed enough to go home.

PLACES

We spent summer afternoons at Holmes Lake, which was green as radiator fluid and emitted a fishy whiff when the wind blew across it.

We spread our towels on the gravelly beach, anchoring each corner with a shoe, or book, or can of Tab. We rubbed Coppertone over our arms and legs and lay back. Sun poured from the sky. Canoers laughed from the middle of the lake. In the distance, children shouted.

We lay with our eyes closed, close enough so that if you wanted to tell me something, all you had to do was slide your fingers across your towel and tap the back of my hand. I'd turn, shading my eyes, and you'd say something funny—it was long enough after the trouble had been taken care of that your sense of humor had returned—and I'd smile and then close my eyes and we'd continue to tan.

Boys drifted over. They lifted handfuls of sand and released thin streams of it over our legs, teasing us until we sat up, made eye contact, and swatted their hands away.

COLLEGE

Of course we rented an apartment together: we were best friends. We walked to school in the morning, dissecting the boys we dated. *Why they are the way they are* was a subject of endless speculation. Why did they do, or fail to do, certain things in bed? Why didn't we simply tell them what we liked? After all, we told each other.

At night we finished our homework, and then went to bars downtown: Sandy's, Cliff's, Barrymore's. On weekends, we walked to the Drumstick to hear bands. In each place, we had a particular table where we liked to sit. People always knew where to find us.

THINGS WE BELIEVED

A car with one headlight out meant someone would want to kiss one of us later in the evening. Body heat eliminated wrinkles, so we only ironed the collars and cuffs of our blouses, trusting that the rest of the fabric would warm to smoothness under our Shetland sweaters. You claimed that eating an entire grapefruit after a meal cut the meal's calories in half, so our refrigerator was always stocked with grapefruit.

PLACES

I'd do anything he asked.

That, you said, was the definition of love.

His name was T—. He was older, dark-haired, dark-eyed, an artist. The sort of person I'd expected to be jaded, but he was enthusiastic and curious about things. Together, he and I had little adventures: going for beers in one of the working class bars in Havelock, trying to hop a train, stumbling around in fields after the bars closed and looking for ditchweed. We'd end up back at the apartment, on the living room floor, kissing until we passed out.

T— wanted to climb a grain elevator, the one out by the penitentiary. We were drunk. Late June, close to midnight. (You were busy with your own preoccupations, as I would learn shortly.)

The climb was less difficult than I anticipated, since there wasn't a single scary ladder that went up the side of the elevator. Instead, various short ladders led to little platforms, so the trip up consisted of many small climbs rather than one long one. The top of the elevator was a flat space, probably four foot square, covered with gravel. We stood there, two hundred feet above the ground, looking down at the tiny cars on the highway, the tiny lights of the city, the bunched trees, the fields.

I turned to him. We kissed. Eyes closed, I didn't worry about how close I might be to the edge.

BEST FRIENDS

A week or so after I climbed the grain elevator with T—, you and I were sitting outside the Lincoln Municipal Airport, watching a plane land, when you said, I slept with R—.

R—, I said. You mean your boss? That R—?

You nodded.

Your boss! In the back room of Books and Cameras, after the store closed.

The thing that distinguished R— from others we'd slept with: he was married.

You put your hands over your face. You wanted to know if I thought you were a terrible person.

Of course not, I said. I squeezed your hand to show I didn't feel any differently toward you at all. I only thought it was remarkable how adultery, which had seemed like such a shocking, unthinkable act, was really no big deal, a line you could cross over unmarked.

On the tarmac, the plane rolled to a stop. Dusk began to darken the sky above us. Beyond the airport grounds, fields stretched out, endless.

DANGER

I'd do anything he asked.

T— waited until the forecasters predicted a bad thunderstorm, then he said, Let's go tunneling.

We were driving around in his El Camino, drinking beer. I had to ask what he was talking about. Tunneling meant going down into the storm sewer behind Lincoln General Hospital and walking two miles through the giant concrete pipes—they were so large a grown man, like T—, could stand upright—until they opened into a big field near the penitentiary.

The fact a storm was coming gave the whole enterprise a little kick. We might have to hurry if rain began rushing in the pipes.

So we descended, armed with flashlights and beers. The tunnel was like a narrow room with curved walls, a rounded ceiling overhead. Our footsteps echoed on cement. Other people had been down here; T— swung his flashlight over spray-painted graffiti. *Beware of Dogs. There are Three Versions of the Truth. Don't look back.* A trickle of water flowed down the middle of the floor. We could hear the occasional rumble of cars passing overhead when the tunnel took us beneath a street.

T— waited until we'd gotten far into the tunnel before he said, Stop a minute. He put the flashlights on the floor. He took the beer I was holding out of my hand. I knew what was coming next. It was the first time with him, the only time, one of the last nights I saw him. We kissed while the city moved above us, while unseen storm clouds bunched together in the sky.

Our dropped clothes puddled on the floor. The flashlights cast our shadows moving on the walls. The sounds we made echoed around us. He said my name. He said, You make me crazy. I wish—.

I should have asked, Wish what?

Cement scraped my elbows, the palms of my hands, my knees. The sweat, the tensed muscles, the riveting convulsions, then silence. He bumped one of the flashlights with his foot and it rolled away. After a minute, we got our clothes back on, stood, and continued walking. My legs were sore; the beginnings of bruises throbbed on my spine.

We came to the end of the tunnel and stepped into a field. Clouds overhead, cars rushing in the distance. The air smelled like rain, and after a few moments big drops began to splatter down.

BEST FRIENDS

You said, I think he's the one.

The one? I said. Really?

You sat across the room from me. We'd graduated from college but still lived in the same apartment. I worked for S— Brothers

Realty. You'd started law school and the boy you were talking about was one of your classmates. I'd met him a couple of times when he'd come to pick you up. He was a little younger than we were, blond, husky, literal. Something about him made me think of one of your mother's sayings: A bird in the hand is worth two in the bush.

You sat in the chair you always sat in. I was on the couch. I wanted to ask what, precisely, made you so sure, but then you said, You'd never say anything about what I told you at the airport, would you?

DANGER

Your brother told us that during World War II, when Hitler planned his takeover of the United States, he'd chosen Lincoln to be his center of operations. Because it was the center of the country.

THE WEDDING

In the church. Not yet dusk. Some outside light still bled through the windows, staining our arms and hands. We bridesmaids stood arranged on the steps to the altar, one girl per step, like kids on rungs leading to a diving board so high you might kill yourself by jumping off. I was the maid of honor, the one closest to you in your white dress. I thought that even though you were getting married, nothing would change between us, that you'd call me after the honeymoon and tell me everything he'd said, the new ways he'd put his hands on your body now that you were his wife. There would always be things about you I knew that he wouldn't.

THE PLURAL FIRST PERSON PRONOUN

After you returned from the honeymoon, everything was "we." "We" had a lovely time in Cancun. "We" loved *Heat*. "We" have been working on the thank-you notes (though I knew you were the only one working on them—I saw the stack you mailed out, with every address in your familiar handwriting).

We're sorry—we're so busy.
We're too tired.
We're pregnant.

LEAVING

Sometimes people left—off to grad school, off to jobs somewhere else. They usually came back over the holidays, and they'd turn up in certain places. I'd go to Barrymore's, for instance, and David K— and his friends from high school would be sitting at a table in the corner, punching each other's arms like they probably did when they were twelve years old.

Or at the mall, there'd be familiar faces in the line to sit on Santa's lap, men I'd known as boys, now with wives I didn't know and their babies I'd never seen before.

WHY I STAYED

Because I felt safe here. Because I knew where the streets led. If someone wanted to find me, she'd know where I was.

THE DRESS

You'd been gone for years that morning I drove down Twenty-Seventh Street, past the neighborhood—now seedier—where we had lived in college. I was killing time before the rush of open houses, feeling virtuous at being out early on a Sunday morning, not hungover the way I would have been ten or fifteen years ago.

Oh, the hangovers. Remember how we'd lie around on the floor of the living room, cataloging our discomforts, experimenting with various remedies: combinations of food and aspirin (two tacos and four Bayer extra strength), liquids and exercise (tomato juice and situps)?

Today a scrim of watery clouds diluted the sunlight. A bare few cars moved on the street. I stopped at the light at Twenty-Seventh and Vine and saw two girls on the northwest corner. They were young, in their twenties, I guessed. Pretty, and put together in a way that might make me think they were on their way to church, except for the fact that one stood a couple feet behind the other, and they held a long wrapped object between them. Because the object was wrapped in a sheet, and because it was approximately the size of a body, my first thought was that the girls were carrying a corpse. The body of a friend who'd fallen in the course of a Saturday night. Of course that was a ridiculous notion—I realized as soon as I thought it that it made no sense. But then an edge of the sheet lifted in the breeze, and I saw lace underneath. Lace, and satin—enough weight of fabric to require two bearers. And I realized the girls were carrying a wedding dress. The sheet protected it from dirt. One of them was probably getting married later that afternoon.

The light turned green. I watched the girls in my rearview mirror until I turned left on Holdrege and the angle of the street cut them out of sight.

I wanted to tell you about the incident, how funny my first impression had been. You, on the other hand, would have known immediately that they held a wedding dress. We would laugh about how those perceptions said so much about who we are. But by then I hadn't known your phone number for years.

PLACES

In Barrymore's, I sit at the back corner table with David K—, who's in town for Christmas and wanted to get together for old times' sake. Barrymore's is built into the backstage area of the Stuart Theater, and the ceiling rises a good forty feet above my head. David mostly looks the same, though he's starting to lose his hair. He lives in Montana, and he's divorced now. He still drinks Coors, like he did in high school.

The waitresses in Barrymore's dress in black and white clothing, and that was a little joke you and I had: whenever one of us had on, say, black pants and a white shirt, we'd ask, Do I look too much like I'm going to work at Barrymore's?

David picks at the label on his beer bottle. Why did we break up? he wants to know.

That was a long time ago, I say. I don't remember.

THE PAINTING

Titled *Preparation of the Bride*, the painting by Gustave Courbet radiates a kind of melancholy. The scene is dimly lighted. Women in bustled skirts arrange cloths on tables and sheets on a bed; they kneel to wash the feet of a girl propped on a chair, a girl who must be the bride. In the painting, she holds a mirror in one hand, her head tilts to one side, her eyes appear almost closed.

You would look at the painting and say her eyes are almost closed because she's thinking about the hours ahead, the moment when she will turn to a groom so moved his voice cracks when he says his vows. Her eyes are almost closed with a feeling of bliss and relief at giving up her name and taking his.

THE TRUTH

In truth, Lincoln isn't the precise center of the country. The precise center of the country lies east of town, in the middle of a field. An uninhabited place.

I've also heard that the precise center of the country is a hundred miles south of Lincoln, across the Kansas border, in a town called Lebanon.

The truth is, I always wanted too much.

Another fact: *The Preparation of the Bride* is not the painting's original title. I learned that x-rays done on the painting in the 1960's showed that the central figure—the girl, the bride—was originally nude. The painting's true name was *The Preparation of the Dead Girl*. After Courbet abandoned the piece, unfinished, some later artist took a brush to the naked girl and covered her in a white gown, as if the dress could resurrect her and transform the scene into one of hope and possibility.

A woman kneels at the girl's feet and another stands at the back of the chair, both poised to lift her the way they'd brace themselves to lift a body.

Maybe you'd be able to convince me that the gathered women aren't in mourning, that the somber light means only that it's too early for sun. But I know the white dress Courbet's bride wears isn't enough to bring her back to life. The mirror she holds close to her face shows no condensation from living breath. She is dead, the way you are now, in some sense, dead to me.

FIELDS

This is how I remember you: we're young, it's summer. We lie down in green fields, on top of quilts our grandmothers made, beneath the bodies of boys who are the sons of the sons of the sons of the men who founded this city. Overhead, stars crowd the sky. Locusts hum in the weeds. Our movements disturb soil beneath the quilt so that some rises as dust and enters our lungs as we breathe. It becomes part of us as we will one day become part of this land, along with the bones of Indians who once lived here, the bones of their ponies.

Acknowledgments

Thanks to the editors in whose magazines some of these stories first appeared. My gratitude also to the teachers I've had at the University of Nebraska and North Carolina State University, and to my fellow students in workshops, who have offered wise counsel. Thanks to Wilton for bringing me into the Wolfpack. Credit goes to Marvin Hunt for help with certain details in "Dr. Faustus in Lincoln." Thank you, Angela, for making us write metafiction! Ted, you were right about "Three Versions of the Truth." And kudos to Jill, the consummate structural problem-solver. I am grateful to Kevin and Sheryl for their support and enthusiasm. A hearty toast to old friends Brad and Julie. None of these stories would have been written without the influence of the muses, who have visited in the form of Chloe, Beth, Yogi, Emma, Lucille, Haley, and Scout. Finally, big thanks to my husband, John McNally, who has been ceaselessly encouraging and has enriched my life in many ways; "I'd tip my hat to you, but I haven't got a hat."

About the Author

AMY KNOX BROWN is a native of Lincoln, Nebraska. She received a BFA in creative writing from Stephens College, MA and PhD degrees in English and creative writing from the University of Nebraska, a JD from Nebraska's College of Law, and most recently, an MFA in creative writing from North Carolina State University. Her fiction, poetry, and creative nonfiction have appeared in *Shenandoah, The Missouri Review, Other Voices, Meridian, Crab Orchard Review, American Literary Review, Witness, the Nebraska Review, Beloit Fiction Journal, Spoon River Poetry Review*, and *Narrative Magazine*, as well as many other literary journals, and in the anthologies *Times of Sorrow/Times of Grace: Writing by Women of the Great Plains-High Plains* (Backwaters Press, 2002); *The Student Body: Short Stories about Life in the University* (Univ. of Wisconsin Press, 2001); and *High Infidelity: 24 Great Short Stories about Adultery by Some of Our Best Contemporary Authors* (William Morrow, 1997). Ms. Brown is the 2005 winner of NCSU's Brenda L. Smart Prize for short fiction (judged by Lee Smith) and the 2006 winner of NCSU's Brenda L. Smart Fiction prize (judged by Shannon Ravenel). Other honors include the Mari Sandoz/*Prairie Schooner* Prize for Fiction, the Vreelands Award, a Henfield Prize, the Louise Pound Fellowship, and a Bread Loaf Writers' Conference scholarship. She is an Assistant Professor of Creative Writing and English at Salem College, where she directs of the college's new creative writing major.

About our Cover Artist

PIVI MOLINGHEN lives in Belgium, and his work can be found online at www.Pivi.be. A close friend had this to say about him (translated from French by Danielle Tarmey):

"Pivi is a man who moves along calmly with a sense of tranquility. He has a piercing look that conveys the discerning, clairvoyant philosopher that he is.

"Loyal in friendship, he can be disarming to those who get to know him because he has two sides: at times austere or fun-loving, at times simple or perfectionist, at times composed or tormented…

"A die-hard humanist, inquisitive about everything, his passion for photography is inversely proportionate to his desire to walk everywhere.

"If he is sleeping, don't wake him—he is thinking!"

Pivi can be contacted at info@pivi.be

Printed in the United States
93792LV00001B/352-408/A